Erosions of Death

Vanae Echoes

Erosions of Death

iUniverse books may be ordered through booksellers or by contacting:

iUniverse
1663 Liberty Drive
Bloomington, IN 47403
www.iuniverse.com
1-800-Authors (1-800-288-4677)

Because of the dynamic nature of the Internet, any web addresses or links contained in this book may have changed since publication and may no longer be valid. The views expressed in this work are solely those of the author and do not necessarily reflect the views of the publisher, and the publisher hereby disclaims any responsibility for them.

Any people depicted in stock imagery provided by Thinkstock are models, and such images are being used for illustrative purposes only. Certain stock imagery © Thinkstock.

ISBN: 978-1-4620-1382-1 (sc)
ISBN: 978-1-4620-1383-8 (e)

Print information available on the last page.

iUniverse rev. date: 12/07/2017

Contents

Chapter 1

The enigma

A thousand darkened roses blossomed within both palms of his most inner hands. He smiled so bright that the earth sounded of steady yielding rhythmic lapse begging of mercy. A lost soul yearning for belonging, stared deeply into the pits of his eyes, hoping for a living sense of delicateness, but only to find a quantum of screeching kayos. When he spoke to her, she felt his atmospheric tongue melt onto his breath. Expelled mists reached the back of her neck like a shadow beneath a non-leveled existence, and the taste of his sorrow for her was short and bitter as salivated poisons. The emotions she shared with him ran deep of a witty turbulence full of utter turmoil and stray walls that shook as they stood beside, keyed, pressed on to her every sway. Her words for him were hesitant and withered.

Many times over and again, blazing, trickling tears fell full from fires of lust. She'd been leashed by him. As he plunged into her flesh, his name possessively burnt the skin. He spoke to her in many dimensions of transparent greed, and desperation blackened his heart. Sarah's mornings awakened short and murmured with bliss of diluted air that suffocated her surroundings. The songs of rejoicing in praise, of which birds sing to the sweet softness, were no longer harmonized in her presence. It was nothing and just noise to the tunneled ear.

The distant sun near the off-setting of rays appeared heart wrenching beyond reach of imaginative ability that stretched along as she dazed into the sky; awaiting for a parallelism between the two unleveraged worlds that exist outside her limits.

Sarah could not quite understand why her husband Fabian did not demonstrate the type of affection she gave onto him, that he once gave in return. Sarah continued on to serve Fabian as her daily routine, with a hint of ginger just beside his tea that she ever so perfectly stirred. While the moment last, Sarah greeted Fabian off to his day in a refreshing tone, only to hear in return the quietness of silence as he left Sarah to her choirs. The sensation of calming winds blew through her hair once again as she stood at the front door entrance, with burgundy silk to her feet. She gasped for a fresh breath of air, to feel emptiness, solid of inner pitted weakened cries to the stomach. As she picked her head from her shoulders, in the moment of disparity; she'd envisioned herself transcending into the clouds in angels' way and leaving all troubling conditions behind. She then shut the door before returning to the kitchen of the secluded mansion that had become like one of a locked prison.

On this particular day, she observed every tiny structured and detailed occurrence as a layout in her little journal, delicately wrapped in pink ribbons that reminded her of the soft love she once experienced with Fabian. Turning each page of the scrambled past, as she concentrating deeply on her emotions and perceptions in means of belonging in comparison to time. As she furthered along in the little journal, she smelled fresh roses as she lay in the fields of forever yielding flowers, and the sun prickled the tip of her nose, escaping for the moment. She began to lift her ink pen to predict the norms of event that is to transpire on this particular day. Her insights were pretty well crafted and precise, finding peace within herself to include that it will eventually be interrupted.

Once more, she returns to drift into her thoughts and effectuating over them. As she thumbed through her little purple journal, she remembered the day her husband had purposed to her on the Caribbean Island, while admiring her sleek body, and standing under a long waterfall that joined into a mountaintop. She remembered the two of them enjoying the loveliest cruise, and sailing across the sea on a virtual horizon hemisphere, as they overcame bumpy currents. Sarah reminisced of the times she would watch the early morning dew mist that linger just between the leveled waters and the sky, awaiting for the sunset to settle into place right over the sea, as if the bottom part of the sun was hiding just below the sea surface. They watched the stars closely and searched for the lighthouse from afar. "Ah!" Sarah thought as she dazed into her little journal. The memoir brought back the photogenic memory of fishing for a degenerated amount of coracles, fish, and grilling lobsters on the edge of the shore. Suddenly, she sadly turned away from her memorable moments for a dose of logic reality. Sarah was more of a naturist individual who enjoyed the simplest things within life's elements. Despite the fact, that her husband Fabian was very in doubtfully stable, not to mention the chief executive in demand of one of the most leading and innovative technology based corporations in the nation, Sarah still enjoyed the simple things out of life.

Fabian was pretty well drawn away from Sarah on the day to day basis, which became the monopoly for them both. Fabian way very comfortable with the way the relationship was structured with Sarah, being that he was arrogant and set in his own ways. While Sarah was sought by her peers to be loving, compassionate and kind to others, Fabian on the other hand, was sought to be of an inferior and invincible type of man in character to be exact.

Despite the fact that Fabian was a rich and greedy man, still half of the company's possessions was to Sarah, royalties, ownership, company profit and capital was all to her. Originally, she'd accompany Fabian with the start-up process of the successful technology company from ground up. Once the company set skyrocket, Fabian took over all the presidential responsibilities of the company, in which Sarah was left with very little insights on the operations of the company after a while. Fabian had a generously less amount o f skills it took to properly manage a business than Sarah, but he always maintained to refuse her assistance and hold back certain financial functions. Clearly, Fabian wanted to over dominate Sarah to her greatest ability. In Sarah's gut, there lays a suspicion of foul play in Fabian's work role, and even thinks that he may be tapping into the account systems of stockholders and investors. Deep down, Sarah questions the true merit of her marriage based on Fabian's faultiness. Sarah knows that the man she's become to know, love, trust and marry would never do anything in this nature, but her confusion continues to hunt her from day to day. Now her means of perceptions to their relationship is twisted and unrevealing. The possibility of Fabian using Sarah for his own personal financial gain is in question at this point.

The fear that lives on in Sarah's heart form day on is the matter of if she'd indeed committed to, and married the wrong man after-all. If she finds this to be so, this only means that she now has a huge situation on her hands both financially and emotionally. None of these conditions can she tolerate being flushed down the toilet after all of her hard work and dedication she invested in getting the company up and running. Sarah attempted to address Fabian's faultiness in the past, but She could never quite validate her intuitions factual concern about Fabian, and it only seemed to have pushed Fabian further to a distance in their relationship than before.

As she sits at home alone, her challenging temptations to disport from the secluded scenery slowly and surely vanishes away from clear thought. The love she had for Fabian was so strong, so greatly admired, and in return, so dreadfully dead. Many years of hoping to build love's harmony had played its taking in death.

She thinks to herself "so much of giving all of me and not an appreciation, not a soft touch, nor a just kiss". She thinks of all the right reasons to be dismissed and freed like a bird in the wind. How she yearns to be renewed from her limp and lonely self.

Escaping for the moment, she reflects in her journal as a quick and easy get-away. Reminiscing of the times she felt alive in her spirit and pleased in her heart. She then begins to trip back to the times when Fabian showered her with love and affection around the time they first met, "Those were the best times of all." She thinks and remembers of how happy Fabian once was when he very first committed himself into marriage; it had not been very long ago. Sarah begins questioning herself" where did the love ever go to?"

Reality settles in harder than solid rocks and she knows it's time to put her journal away for the day to tend to her choirs, that he will eventually show again with an empty facial expression that hardened the sight and which told a long gathering of life-long unwashed mysteries. She'd watched the morning sun die down into evening, then the relevant stars in the sky shined just of dimly enough to sustain a thought for the second in peace, she'd found in the early day alone.

His heart is hallowed and withered for her as night until oblivious eternity. Exploded blood vessels from anger are visible with his planted shoes in the middle of the floor, boasting on. Soon with a throws of his head, all buildings will be of a useless monument. With a point of a finger to ensure her that she is beneath his authoritarian command, and rambling on about her imperfect competence in comparison to his prior love in marriage. Sarah's tied and limp body rested at the edge of the sofa as she heard Fabian's voice echoing in her ear, "Your incompetence is of a disgrace to me, pick your face up from the floor. You've never come in compliance with my rules around here, (He continued torturing Sarah) only if Vanessa was still here you'll have no say so." So on to say, Vanessa was his first wife before he took Sarah's hand into marriage. During the last days Vanessa remained married to Fabian, one day she passed away peacefully in her sleep. Vanessa was a kind-hearted spirited woman and brought many bright days to Fabian, well so far as he claimed! All day long, Fabian would ramble on about the times shared amongst him and Vanessa, even to spare the details of their explicit most passionate steamy sex-life to Sarah, but as usual, Sarah remained silent under his eagle eye of pervasion.

He continued to belittle Sarah every day of their lives together, saying Vanessa this…Vanessa that and sending Sarah on a verge of nervous state of a mental break in shock. He'd discussed ludicrous to Sarah as in how luscious and tender Vanessa's bosoms were in comparison to her own. Only if Sarah was a true believer that breast implants would solve the problems they were experiencing in their marriage, she'd do just about for Fabian. But she truly believed that improvement of her body figure alone wouldn't retrieve the love she'd lost, and to despite the fact that he was obviously a very manipulative and filthy husband to be exact. Sarah's faith in him to change was almost worth nothing. When Sarah looked into his eyes, she'd sense all of his pellucid dirty secretes he'd kept when he stepped away from her site.

The sound of thunder on rainy nights was yet not insuring of plentiful crop, but yet, a reminder of harsh, extended footsteps, as devastating as spears glazing the heart at every intermitted electrode heartbeat. Each raindrop was a reflection of Sarah's tears following into the puddle that follow it. The sound of flowing waters were no longer peaceful, but a distraction under absurdly loud vowels. Sarah reflected on her silhouetted identity, searching for just a tiny piece of beauty left in her skin, digging so deeply to the bone, and past the course of her interior design. She combed her fingers through her fiery red hair, puckered her lips and gently patted her pale cheeks tightly, loosing herself in her presents of absences. She critically examined every inch on her body until she'd reached mental exhaustion. Sarah was really a beautiful woman inside and out, but when she dazed into the mirror at her big brown eyes, she saw nothing in her presence to define as worthy.

Every morning she began t reflect on her image as she talked aloud of herself in criticism when Fabian was away. She thought of how perfect Vanessa must have been to Fabian, and wondered what made her so distinctively different. Poor Sarah never had anyone to consult about her personal matters on hand, especially with the maintenance of polishing Fabian's "perk" reputation. Sarah was more of a uniquely self-reserved person, who was always known for her elegance, independence and gleaming personality, just up until a few months ago when Fabian suddenly lost his entire interest in Sarah all together.

From day to day, Sarah quantified the love still possessed of her in Fabian, as she admired the virtuousness in the bouquet of white roses that posed the only most-gentle living element in her atmosphere. And every day, Sarah escaped in her little purple journal for the moment until it was time for Fabian to return home. Every day of her life was as a well-rehearsed script to prediction, exactly accordingly, and loneliness began to settle in harder than rock bottom pits of emptiness.

So much of agonizing pains, hurtful stares, demeaning eyes, crushed feelings, Sarah was drifting away. Not even measurably drastic statistics couldn't bring poor Sarah back, not even with the highest quality dose of a concentrated cure. From here, there was no turning back. Sarah was numb. Every breath of hope vaporized past existence, and she began t feel a transitioning pushing through slowly but surely as hours pasted.

Fabian returned home on this day with the same grouched ordering look on his face as he did everyday while Sarah continued to serve onto him. He sat down in his black leather ottoman and plopped his feet on top, pointing to his service table in an imperious way. As Sarah presented herself to him, he'd notice something different in Sarah and could not distinguish what it might have been. But all together, the thought of her just discussed him to his mid-section of his form. So, he accepted her service and shunned her off from his complete sight. That night, sounds of beastly waves moved within Sarah, shaking her flesh, sparing affection not, and deliverance of torture Fabian gave as he envisioned Vanessa.

Fabian woke up the next morning with Vanessa on his mind, smothering his thoughts of how he used to cater to Vanessa with bed and breakfast, including the deserts form the previous night. He turned over to see Sarah's tiny sleek body and pulsating veins from her forehead, and that was enough to turn him off more than he could tolerate as he jumped out of bed. That morning, Sarah wept and strangled her voice under her soaked pillow-case before returning to composure. After seeing Fabian off to work, Sarah cleansed herself from his despicable dirt lubricant, as she felt below matted filth that he'd walked on. Sarah thought she was in need of some fresh air, for she felt intoxicated over his suffocating polluted aromas that slept beneath the lower layer of her skin and lingered the air. She began to reflect on the penetrated hate that had taken its part in the taking of her soul; knowing that it had been months since he'd shown the least bit of interest in her. "Maybe his unknown mystery mistress refused him attention last evening before deciding to return him home perhaps." She thought.

Collecting flowers were part of Sarah's adult onset rewarding since she was a young adolescent. She stood in the corner of the garden near the stoned bird bath, as she felt the delicateness of a wildflower. She, herself did not feel very attractive for a very long time now, just as something pure being exposed to deadly toxins. She whiffs the scent of the flower as she thought of how it reminds her of the way she used to feel…alive, young and beautiful. Butterflies pranced around the flowers and the cool air sooth Sarah's skin. Sarah led her feet along the marble stone path to the bird feeding area as her shadow followed closely behind, with the sun shyly hidden behind the clouds. The birds blushed back at Sarah as the wind rippled their reflections in the birdbath, then they snickered in amusement at her slight twinkle from the sun, tickling Sarah's skin before flying away in the fresh breeze of slight wind. The tiny sparkles of sunshine were of a greater quantity of light than the happiness left in her soul.

Sarah came to terms with herself to leave her peaceful scenery from within the garden, and return inside the house to tend to her choirs. Sarah gathered her gardening tools and slowly stepped back inside the home. Sarah suddenly become confused and forgotten what she had entered back into the hose for. She became a bit over-whelmed and consulted with herself once more in the mirror, splashing water on her face from the bathroom faucet. As she picked her head out of the face bowl, she began asking herself aloud, "Who am I, What's happening to me?" The question penetrated into her mind so deeply that she became lost in her confused facial expression. Microseconds, then minutes passed and there she was still plotted in front of the mirror with the same confused expression. "How can I make things right with Fabian once again?" Sarah found herself in the bathroom she share with who she thought of once to love her the same as she love him, but now, he's as a stranger or even an enemy in her own home and bed in which she rest.

Sarah looked over Fabian's business attire that hung perfectly in the closet and wondered what happened to the time lapse form when love was alive and now, from the person he once was, to the person he'd become to be? She wondered if she could ever get back into his heart or even his min, for he was another person, and more withdrawn every day. She searched over his belongings for any lead-way to fully expose the person he turned out to be. Just a clue would be just enough to allow her to get inside the realms of his world, but there was nothing that refreshes her mind. She observed the cufflinks on the cuffs of his executive pressed suit, to the shined and polished dress shoes in his preference. Their wedding picture lay on the dresser shattered near the necklace given to her as a gift from him on their first anniversary earlier on in the previous year. Everything he possessed was no longer familiar to Sarah, and she was lost. The more she searched, the further she became confused. The more she became attached to him, the further he pushed her away to deny her of the love she held for him.

Sarah remembered one of the reasons for her leaving the garden and returning into the house, it was to gather the bleeding heart roots from last year pillaring around Valentine's Day that she had planted for herself. She began to wonder why her husband occupied her mind ninety percent of the time other than the fact of him being her husband. Sarah was once the president of a magazine publishing company in New York. After Sarah and Fabian became married, he persuaded her to resign from her career path to stay home, and to become a homemaker t the child they never had. Now, Sarah's only hobbies include tending to her flourishing flower garden in her greenhouse, especially now since Fabian completely disregarded Sarah from the technological company that she started. Sarah had repeatedly expressed to Fabian her desires to open her own flourishing boutique from home, but nothing from Sarah ever seemed to spark his interest at the least bit. Sarah searched within herself for an answer to her own question, why she made such a poor quality of a judgment decision to excuse her life as a today's leading business woman, and ridding of her status quo in the magazine industry, along with her friends and family? Now she is dead to the world and even to her most beloved husband.

From months and months, Sarah and Fabian had tried to introduce a new addition into their family, but they never saw it happen. Sarah wondered if her not being able to conceive was the root formation for Fabian's distant attitude. Sarah never had the guts to confront Fabian of this, just knowing that every time she lost herself in his presence, the disgusted look across his face was of a defense mechanism to avoid him sharing his thoughts and feelings with Sarah.

From time to time, Sarah would fantasize about visiting the local grocery store for a fresh stock of meats and vegetables for the souse, but she'd mostly go for bread and butter, tea, honey and ginger for Fabian's morning tea. She most certainly enjoyed to window shop for the latest flowers and plants to add to her enormous collections in her fresh garden. Her array of flowers varied form a wide range of roses to cactus, and Lilly pads in cater to the frogs that hopped form one Lilly to the next near the tiny pond just below the water fountain.

Sarah found that all of her choirs were completed and she decided to take an aromatherapy soaking in her and Fabian's hot tub. She began to gather her luxurious collection of oils and candles then plan them to the side. She began meditating over her expensive China cabinet that was given to her as an inheritance gift by one of her great aunts from Paris just right after the passing of her mother. The China cabinet was filled with gifts from close friends and family members during her and Fabian's marriage ceremony; including their memorable wedding glasses, that sat on the top shelf in an inspiring and uplifting spirit sort of way. Sarah opened the glass cabinet and took out one of the glasses, then headed towards the wine and champagne cooler. She then elevated up into the master bedroom, grabbing her microfiber spa robe and slippers before entering into the bathroom. Sarah choose the most expensive and fresh towels to begin her relaxation moment, then arranged the candles in sequence as they were on the last day she could remember Fabian joining in on the bubbly and steamy soak. Sarah poured honeydew milk into the bubbly hot tub and began her soaking with her glass of Crystal Brut, "Methuselah" on a tiny bit of crushed rocks.

As Sarah soaked her tired body, she felt the warmth of the water soothing her completely internally. She dipped her head under the bubbles to feel the relief from head to toe and through every pore of her entirely. She stared at herself in the mirror that was of the ceiling in this once romantic scenery, and for some reason, she'd wish she were Vanessa. She thought of all the affection and attention she would receive if she could only know how it felt to be her. She began wondering how she looked and act that was so different from her own. She wondered what she'd worn when Fabian would come home from a long days of work, and Sarah became obsessed in the moment as she sipped her bubbly champagne.

Fabian returned home to find Sarah in the Jacuzzi. "What are you trying to do, stir up memories of Vanessa?" "Just relaxing" Sarah answered. "Well, I think it is time for you to get out." Fabian paid Sarah no attention as he left form the bathroom to tend to his late dinner that had been waiting for him in the microwave. Sarah then entered into the lounging area where Fabian was sitting and picked up a magazine, hoping she could spark a conversation of any sort. Fabian asked, "What is that scent?" "What darling, (Sarah replied as she pierced into Fabian's slanted eyes) is it not clean enough in here for you/' "No, it's not that. It's just that you smell…" Sarah interrupted. "Do I smell breath-taking like Vanessa or not?" Fabian searched over Sarah in a shocking manner, as he wondered what type of prank Sarah was up to. He began to think that perhaps Sarah had just gotten a hold of some type of new scent from her flower garden, for it was the exact same scent of the perfume Vanessa worn every day when she was alive. "How do you know" Fabian asked, but Sarah had no words for him and looked at Fabian in a deceitful way, with a slight crack of a blush written on her face, as she slowly excused herself away from Fabian's sight and saying to him, "You look as if you've seen a ghost!" Fabian replied with anger risen in his voice, "Have you bought any new flowers or greeneries lately Sarah?" But Sarah refused to respond as she held the peak of her nose high towards the sky; splashing Fabian in the face with her long wet hair, leaving him in suspicion. Other than Vanessa's picture he'd kept securely locked away in a secret safe, he could not remember any of Vanessa's personal belongings being left behind with him; he was for sure he'd remember , especially something so obvious as her perfume. He was puzzled beyond his predictions, but he shortly came to the conclusion to begin lusting over Vanessa as usual in his mind.

That night, Fabian held Vanessa's picture closely to him as he dazed into the ceiling with Sarah in presence. Fabian had experienced the finer things in life and his super-ego led him to believe he was of a godly image to his peers in his own damned and pathetic world. He thought of himself to be above all others, with the rest of the world to his knees of services and pleading as he abused his authority. When ever and whatever he says always went his way. Fabian found his self clouded with the smell of Vanessa on Sarah, and engraved in Sarah's the name of Vanessa once again that night. Heaps of lustful fires possessed in his eyes and burned beneath her skin, splitting the pores wide open, and engaging of her thoughts not.

The next morning, Fabian couldn't help but to focus his attention of the scent still left in the pillow sheet that lay on his side of the bed. "That scent is so lovely to my senses. Why must you be so pathetic Sarah? Do you think that by you smelling like Vanessa will make me love you anymore? I'm going to work, and when I get back home, I want that scent gone." Sarah truly did not understand exactly what Fabian was referring to by "perfume", for Sarah had not altered nor add any particular flourishing fragrances to her at all. Despite Fabian's tone, in which she was pretty well adjusted to, she actually saw this new fragrance as a lead way to gain Fabian's blackened heart back in some strangely odd way. Sarah over-shadowed everything Fabian said to her about getting rid of the scent and instead uses this to desperately regain his love.

So, from day one, Sarah started her day in the greenhouse and ended her day in the bubbly jacuzzi, while enjoying a fresh glass of Methuselah as she stared into the ceiling mirror, wishing she were Vanessa and her obsession un- expectantly grew stronger by the day. Fabian was enraged from day on not because Sarah had fallen short of completing her daily choirs including dinner preparations, but because of the fact that Sarah still was of the fragrance of Vanessa fierce Fabian until his gritted teeth ripped inner sparks of hatred.

Chapter 2

The awakened revenge

Sarah contemplated in her garden wondering where could have the fragrance really come from? With repetitive ambition, Sarah's daily routine was extinguished too precisely to sustain the scent. Every bit of her actions was accordingly to the day she discovered the fragrance scent. Every flower she'd touched on that day. She repeated even the tiny footsteps in between that she could remember, she attempted before she'd begin her ritual soaking. She executed everything without flaw in perfection and obsession. Fabian arrived home and Sarah could hear him coming through the entrance door. Sarah hopped out the Jacuzzi and into the down stair area. Fabian was having his normal steak and dinner that Sarah just so happen to remember to prepare on this day. Fabian dropped his knife and fork to the floor with his mouth hanging wide open. Sarah seemed to have made a huge transformation, but Sarah seemed to be unaware of where the change had come from. "You look…" She'd taken the words from his mouth. "Astonishing?" Fabian couldn't believe what his eyes had seen. Sarah intrigued his sight. Sarah's hair was silkier than fine silk, her voice had risen to seductive levels, and her body toned to perfection that enticed Fabian. His broad and narrow tongue slaver her neck. Suddenly, the thought of dinner left his complete mind and Sarah was pleased. "Whatever have you done with yourself, you should do more often."

Fabian went on about his day boasting and bragging about Sarah's transformation. He'd shared the news to his pervasive colleagues, friends and family. Everyone he'd come across to share this information with was shocked to death as they mocked Sarah's character. Fabian left from work earl on this day to return home to Sarah, thinking about the previous day of pleasure she'd given to him. Sarah was home soaking in the luxurious Jacuzzi. She'd dipped her head under the water, then came up to see a new her in the mirror with all lit candles as they romantically flickered throughout the dark room. The candles blew out immediately. Later, Fabian came home to find Sarah talking to herself in the water. "What's gotten into you?" Get yourself dress, we're having company shortly." Some of our old friends from the job are coming by for dinner. Why don't you prepare some pate as complimentary ordure for our guest? They'll love it Sarah." Sarah not knowing, that many of the guest that were invited to dinner was only there to make a mockery of Sarah even further; Sarah stepped into her slippers and began just as Fabian asked of her.

Sarah thought the gathering was a bit unusual and out of the ordinary to suspect Fabian's faultiness. Sarah over-heard whisperings, it was coming from one of Fabian's female colleagues who were passing along a compliment to her new appearance to Fabian. Fabian observed Sarah being a bit unusually flirtatious towards one of the men at dinner, but he paid it no mind. Mostly everyone who had appeared on the short notice was a familiar face to Sarah, all except one lady in particular who seemed to have come clear out of nowhere. Sarah wondered if this had been the mystery mistress whom Fabian had been seeing on late nights away from home. Sarah decided to engage in on a conversation with this woman. "My name is Sarah, Fabian's wife. And you are?' "Karen. How do, you do?' "You know, Fabian has told me a lot about you and how well you tend to your garden. You know

Fabian tends to a lot back at the office, and he does a very well job at it as well." "Yes, I can imagine, and I bet you know Sarah approached Fabian and said t him, "I really wasn't prepared for this moment. I'm really exhausted. I must excuse myself right at this moment." 'You're the reason for our guest Sarah. Why ruin the moment?" "What...a moment of your flashiness for what? You're already the most successful man here. What more do you want?" Fabian agreed with approval.

Later that night as Sarah and Fabian lay in the bed, Sarah revisited the dinner gathering and remembered that Fabian had mentioned that everyone had come to see her" as she placed Karen's face with her name once again. '[Who is Karen?" "Owe, Karen is just the office errand girl." "Then, why was it so important for you to invite her to the occasion?' "I don't know, I just thought it would be a nice thing to do since I was inviting everyone else from the office." "Well, if you don't know already, I am not a showcase for your corrupted, white-collar thieves you call friends to see." Every day, Sarah soaked in the Jacuzzi to relax, as she admired her Vanessa-like-figure in the ceiling mirror. Fabian would come home to realize that dinner had not been yet prepared, for he appreciated a punctual service schedule. Fabian rushed up to the bathroom to see what had been holding her, to find again, Sarah talking aloud of herself. "What has become of you, and who are you talking to Sarah?" Sarah replied, "Sarah is not here right now!" "Cut the bull-cap. Get out of the tub right now!" Sarah got out of the tub and followed Fabian down the hall and into the kitchen. "Just forget, I'll order out tonight. Don't wait up." "Where are you going? You're going to visit with your whore Karen?" "What am I to do? You know exactly how I am feeling. What, you call yourself trying to get back at me?" "Just leave as you normally do Fabian, it really doesn't matter anymore."

Because Fabian had became to realization with himself, he'd become addicted to the person she had become. Only he'd noticed something truly different about the way Sarah had changed and even the way she was acting lately. Strangely odd, it was alike an act Vanessa would pull when she was alive. Fabian decided to stay home on this day instead. Owe truly, Vanessa was a sweet by nature person, but she was also a hard driven woman and quiet dominant over Fabian after a while. When it came to taking orders from him, she had built up intolerance. To Fabian, Vanessa was everything but he too tempted her as is does with Sarah. Because of Vanessa's dominant ways, Fabian seemed to treat her like a hierarchy statue. Fabian indeed had a little dirty secret that no one had known of about Fabian's character except Vanessa. When he looked into Vanessa's eyes all he saw of her was his polluted thoughts of sexual images. Through Fabian's eyes, the change in Sarah was of Vanessa's bodily figure that he began to honor in Sarah.

When Fabian was away, there was a conversation amongst Sarah, and whom she thought was the image of Vanessa's. But Fabian never knew of this up until one day when Fabian began to put two into two. "You're obsessed with concept of my heart still being deeply in-love with Vanessa aren't you? And you wish you were her. Don't you?" "You are so sickly twisted Sarah, and I'm afraid you'll need some serious counseling with your identity crisis you're experiencing. You can never be Vanessa, so get over it." The same night, Sarah sat in the Jacuzzi, tipsy from her glass of champagne. She dazed deeply into the mirror at her face glistening in the water as she called, "Vanessa? Vanessa, come… Do you hear me? Vanessa?" Sarah sat in the tub for hours at a time until the skin on her feet gathered and she was ready for bed. Sarah entered into the bedroom and raised the sheets back as she slid into the bed with Fabian's back turned away from her. He felt an absence in Sarah's being and the presence of something or someone else. This instinct feeling he had consumed brought on the hardened goose bumps under the hairs to his back. Fabian could hardly sleep one moment none that night not knowing who Sarah had become. The guilt of how he'd treated her ran through his head without stop as the sweat ran from his pores all that night in suspicion of whom he was actually sleeping with.

The following day, Fabian recognized how Sarah began to act out of the ordinary. It was as Sarah had become a stranger in her own house. She'd refused to tend to her own garden; house errands and choirs just did not seem to exist to Sarah any longer, and Fabian noticed how Sarah suddenly began to wear an unexceptional amount of make-up. Her features had made a transition, not just her body figure alone, but also her facial features as well, as though she was transitioning into someone else's body. Her egotistic personality was not of her. Fabian had notice the engorgement of her bosoms over night. He was a sucker for the anatomy of a woman's structure. Fabian quietly sat back and watched the transformation in Sarah from day to day as the table had turned in the development. Fabian witnessed the dysfunctional turn point that had affected their family's life in which he originally created. All-together, everything was quickly going down the drain. Fabian was curious to lead his feet down into the lounging area where he thought Sarah would be waiting. From the corner of the second hall leading to Sarah, he could see the reflection laying in the middle of the marble floor as she stood perfectly still draped in a white gown near the bar table. He began to as Sarah, "You now those times we attempted to bring a child into the world? In your heart…sometimes, do you still want to have a family with me?" There was a long silence from Sarah… She began to laugh hysterically non-stop. Fabian face was red as a cherry and he asked in an embarrassing tone, "My god Sarah. What's gotten into you?" Sarah hilariously chocked on the last of her laughs she had left in her. "I'm sorry Fabian but I thought you cared to ask." Sarah proceeded to amuse herself by his question.

Fabian began to beg of Sarah's affection from this day on as he was reminding of the love he shared with Vanessa. Sarah knew it was only Vanessa that Fabian saw in her and she refused Fabian until he cried to her feet. When she finally gave in to him, he'd allowed her to take total control. She manipulated his mind and soul with her tools, his lustful thoughts and dirty secretes took him completely.

Sarah knew of Fabian's porn addiction that he took to work with him daily. He was pathetic and inconspicuously useless to her. After leaving work and returning home, Fabian overheard Sarah saying, "This bitch hair is way too long and red. When is the last time this whore has had a hair cut?" Fabian dropped beyond the sounds behind the closed door. He snatched open the door and Sarah was still holding the pair of scissors in her hands with chunks of red hair in her palms and whacked everywhere onto the floor. Fabian stood at the door with his eyes glued wide open, but not a word followed form his mouth and Sarah slammed the door in his face. Fabian had indeed noticed how Sarah had become unbelievably unfamiliar with herself, and how much of a challenge it had become for her to find her way around the mansion like an unconquerable enigma for her. Even knowing this, Fabian still have Sarah the initiative ability to wear his pants and in charge of the mini mansion for a while due to his weakness now to Sarah; in which was the only way he can revisit the memories of Vanessa, is through Sarah.

Sarah headed downstairs to find her husband sitting at their dining room table, eating a large stuffed potato alone as his supper. Sarah said to him, "Honey, get dressed, we're having a guest tonight. Fabian didn't question Sarah the least bit, not this new person in Sarah or anything she'd previously said or done. He simply just got dressed and waited patiently in the lounging area in suspicion of this guest was Sarah is expecting. Around seven-thirty that evening, a gentleman arrived at the footstep and rung the door bell. Sarah opened the door and in came the man who had been patiently waiting by the outside entrance door. At the surprise to Fabian, the young man was the fiancé of one of the guest who had been announced the night of the dinner party. "Stacey! Fabian says, "I didn't expect to see you here. What's the occasion?" Stacey responded, "Well, you know I have a very rich in doubt uncle in France, whom possesses eight-teen flourishing company's, famously known all around the world! Since Sarah has expressed her interest in this type of business, I thought it'd be a wonderful idea if she'd consulted with my uncle. "But Sarah, you haven't even paid your garden any attention in weeks." "You have no say so in this Fabian. My intentions were not to ask of your acceptance. I've made up my mind." Sarah gave Fabian the most betrayal and deceitful of looks as if her eyes could tear every pulsation out of him heart completely dismembered, that even Fabian wanted to jump clearly out of his own skin. "Okay my dear, if this is what you want to do then I'm all for it." "Stacey, would you like a tour around the house?" Sarah asked in an uplifting tone in her voice. Fabian wondered what type of crusade Sarah spawned upon. The tour began in the lounging room and ended in the Jacuzzi room. Sarah knew she was not the least interested in the production or the marketing of a flourishing business.

"Here's the Jacuzzi. This is where Fabian and I use to share but not any longer. He is such a bore" Sarah laughed and then continued with the tour. Sarah envisioned insanely enticing Fabian with her bosoms, then him slavering them. At this point, Sarah was pretty much able to do anything under the sun, as long as Sarah would never leave from Fabian's sight. Sarah escorted Stacey to the door. "You should expect your wife to be missing you by now, right?" Fabian asked Stacey and Stacey replied. "Yes. Yes indeed!" As Sarah closed the door behind the young gentleman, she thought about how she must have gotten under Fabian's skin. Which was exactly part of Sarah's plans – to get into his mind, twisting his heart inside and out wrenching dry?

Chapter 3

Betrayal in silent secrecy

As Fabian sat in the lounging area, Sarah revealed her flawless nakedness to Fabian and he worshiped to his knees. He couldn't see himself without Sarah now. She'd become as a sex-slave to him and his only symbol of Vanessa. Fabian spent seventy percent of his time at work, at his desktop, watching pornography for many of hours in counting; fantasizing about the many tasks and dirty tricks Sarah was to perform for him. The scent of Vanessa whiffed pasted the nostrils of his most recent memory, and only he knows the truth behind the reason for him suddenly hating Vanessa's smell on Sarah. It wasn't because of Sarah's falsifying identity attempt, but really deep down inside in his filthy closet, he knew that the relationship he and Vanessa once had shared together really wasn't as sweet and perfect as he'd portrayed the marriage to be after-all. Too bad Vanessa isn't alive to tell the true story of Fabian and Vanessa's love life!

Believe it or not, Fabian was extensively verbally and sexually abusive towards Vanessa even though he favored deeply in Vanessa because he saw her to have the body of a goddess. Vanessa was once pregnant with Fabian's child until she was six months along, just until she miscarried the child due to stress she'd experienced with

Fabian. Vanessa was a tall, perfectly tanned, slender, and kind-hearted brunette. She was a very attractive e and beautiful woman who went through life with a high ranked reputation; going from high school cheerleader and Victorian to college president and catalog model within one year. Fabian always felt unworthy of her love and became extremely possessive and controlling over Vanessa. He'd forced her to leave her modeling career to remain home throughout the day after stalking her during her photo shoots at each and every set she was call to work.

From day, and through long exhausting days, Fabian had it in for Vanessa. She'd become his homosapien sex-slaved-doll as he said to her, "You posed this way for that Romeo photographer of your, you do as I say." Fabian was overly obsessed with Vanessa, and when it came to sexual orientations, he would never ever, take no for an answer. Whenever Vanessa had told Fabian "no", it seemed to be a threat to his manhood. At the beginning, Vanessa was very vulnerable, helpless and soft-spoken to the disturbing conditions. But eventually, after some time, her mental state of the verbal abuse began to take a toll on her, and she started defending herself against him. She especially enjoyed to triangle around the concepts of reverse psychological techniques. Since he was well known as a sex hobbyist, Vanessa used his own poison against him as the object. Vanessa saw that this was a big weakness of his, along with the fear of actually losing her. So, she continued to played mind-scrambling puzzles with Fabian everyday in return, like a fetch and serve game. Vanessa began to be very violent towards Fabian in return of the abuse she'd experienced. Fabian thought of the abuse as an acknowledgment at this point. Whenever Vanessa snapped her fingers she always got what she'd demanded of him.

Fabian did everything for Vanessa, ranging from the catering of breakfast-in-bed, bubble baths, body massages to candle light dinners at the most fanciest of restaurants in the city. He always felt as though he owed Vanessa to overly spoil her after the abuse, but only to pursue her to stay. And every day, he begged for forgiveness of Vanessa's love over and over again. But, form day out, she demonstrated of how the love she once had for him had demolished. People whom associated with Fabian and Vanessa had not a clue that there was so much abuse going on in the relationship. According to everyone, they had the perfect marriage. One night as Vanessa and Fabian made passionate love, she'd delivered once of the most lustful kisses. She gave onto him and Vanessa fell asleep and never woke from that night. According to Fabian her death was a mysterious. During the autopsy, there was not a trace of mischievous acts on Fabian's part that lead up to the cause of Vanessa's death. So, it was pronounced that she'd passed away peacefully in her sleep.

As Fabian reminisced of the agonizing moment, he wondered if Vanessa had truly passed away because she'd hated him so much that she couldn't bare to love another day with him, and his assumption may have been exactly correct only to an extent. Fabian then returned his focus on Sarah and thinking of all the ways Sarah had drastically changed in only a short amount of time and with all the similarities of Vanessa. But, still deep down inside this still wasn't enough for Sarah to completely please Fabian even if she tried last result. Most of him still wanted Vanessa instead of Sarah, so he fantasized over Vanessa further more. A thought of Sarah broke his concentration once more, and he began wondering how possible was it for Sarah to have underwent such a drastic appearance transformation form just soaking in milk water from home in only a few days? The only logical explanation he could put together was maybe she'd mixed some sort of flowers and oils she'd put together while he was away. He thought that perhaps he should inspire her a bit for some profit of his own, only if he could pursue her into starting a cosmetic company from home. He plotted out how he would present the idea to Sarah once he made it home on this day. He thought to tell her how much he'd forgiven her for the incident that occurred with Stacey. Including him coming to the conclusion that he'd thought about how much he'd deserved the out-come by the way he'd acted like a jerk in front of his friends a colleagues at the dinner party.

Later that early afternoon, Fabian entered in to their mini-mansion shouting, "Sarah! Sarah! I have some wonderful news for you! He started up the stone stairs until he reached the top. He then headed towards the guestroom, where he thought he might have heard Sarah's voice. He had made it halfway to the door, when he stopped right dead in his foot tracks. He'd thought he'd heard an extra voice speaking to Sarah and in response was her voice coming from the guestroom. Fabian observed this extra voice of another woman. He began to gradually approach the door. The back of his mind recollect the fact that Sarah never had any level of interest or the guts to step one single foot inside this room before this moment. He did find it oddly strange that this was the same room Vanessa enjoyed her quiet time and he remembered how much she cherished this room to go meditate when she was alive. Fabian tuned in to the second voice, this voice, a familiar voice to Fabian. Suddenly, the voice toned to a whisper, and he could clearly hear Sarah responding to it. He swung the door open only to find Sarah there alone. "Sarah! What the hell were you just speaking to?" "You'll never know." Sarah cracked a deceitful smile on her face as usual as she responded. "I demand an answer from you Sarah. I demand you to tell me rig ht at this very instant, who in the world were you just speaking to as I approached to open the door and entered into this room?" Sarah smiled in the most disturb way as she responded, "If you must know… I was talking to Vanessa, and she knows how badly you lust for her at work while you sit at your little black desk. She told me this." Fabian's further words were lost past existence, and he took many steps back until her was no longer in the presence of Sarah any longer, leaving her alone to the guestroom.

Fabian became fed-up and decided to speak with his and Sarah family psyche doctor to see if he could have her admitted for metal insanity. The psychologist was very familiar with the complications Fabian and Sarah were having in their marriage, despite the fact that Sarah very seldom consulted with the doctor ever before. When Fabian spoke with the psychologist, he informed Fabian that it wasn't any longer legal to have the ability to admit a spouse or any other adult aged person against their own will; unlike the times when he were married to Vanessa. The psyche doctor included to mention to Fabian that if he could catch Sarah disputing a conversation amongst herself, that the information would be vital and reliably evident in proceeding with the process of having Sarah sent away for a very long time, even against her own will. The psychologist laid his deal out with a high price tag attached, and it was decent enough to offer the doctor a small under-the-table payout for his services. With the riches Fabian possessed, he was more than willing to compromise without further negotiation to proceed.

Fabian decided to secretly tape record the conversation Sarah had been carrying out with herself all alone. He choose the date and time he would step away from this office desk to spy on his wife at home, specifically to ease-drop in on the private conversation she'd held. He crept around the entire mansion until he figured out what room Sarah was in. He found Sarah in the Jacuzzi room where she indeed was found to be talking to herself as if she was engaging in on an enabling journey with another woman as in earlier before. He thought that this location he'd found Sarah in was perfect for the recording devise; since the master bedroom was connected to the Jacuzzi room, he had plenty of time and space for the implantation process in this matrix like room, she seemed to have produced. Fabian could not distinguish the details of the content Sarah whispered about, without him getting caught by Sarah. So, he securely hid the devise and left in confidence.

Fabian stood outside the master bedroom in a duplicitous delight to himself. He was for sure that his plans would work as they were executed exceptionally well when it came to Vanessa, when they were married to each other. Fabian had once made a terrible lie about Vanessa losing her mind, after her attempts to leave him and threatened to give up her hand in marriage to him. Fabian had discreetly committed Vanessa to a mental health facility by convincing the hospital staff she was insane, with the help of Vanessa's formerly known friend, whom Fabian seek for assistance. This friend Fabian consulted t assist with his lie, was a very old friend of Vanessa's and who was also a model like Vanessa. Fabian paid this former friend of hers to be a witness as part o f his evidence in having Vanessa locked away and fraudulently diagnosed as insane. This woman was always under the wings of Vanessa growing up, and was also very envious at the same time, very jealous of the spotlight attention Vanessa had been receiving. This woman, Vanessa's pseudo friend, saw Vanessa's perseverance as endless, her glass as overly poring, while hers seemed very sparing. For that, she wanted everything of Vanessa's possession. That envy grew and the woman eventually had an affair with Fabian the last days of their marriage. This was something that always slept in Vanessa's mind even before it actually occurred.

Sarah finally showed her face out of the bedroom and into the lounging area. "What were you so ever calling me for my darling?' Fabian responded in a mockery type of way, "Owe, honey, I just wanted to talk to you about the development of a new possible fragrance collection for yourself. Would you like that? I think it would be a fabulous thing for you… and you would be diligently successful my love." It is obvious that at this point their relationship was definitely based on lust, betrayal, and revenge from both sides of the table, and both for two different reasons.

Fabian's plans were to figure out Sarah's variables to her discovered scent, and to develop more a modern edition for a new fragrance. He planned to keep Sarah around the house just long enough for her to reveal this to him before having her locked away and labeled as "insane". Guilt ate away at him and he was afraid that Sarah, or anyone for that matter, would find out about the truth behind the way Vanessa was treated by him. Sarah had indeed shared with Fabian some elements of her mixture. Fabian was now more than willing to proceed in having Sarah silently hospitalized against her will for good. But just as before, Sarah was not positively sire that the ingredients were accurately correct, or even closely linking at all to the scent in which stuck to her skin.

Fabian anxiously anticipated on presenting the hard-core evidence to the psyche doctor to have her gone for good. Sarah didn't mind at all for Fabian stepping away from the home, in which he told him that he was going back to the office to finish some last minute work that will come due soon. Instead, Fabian was in and out of the doctors home as fast as if he had never made an appearance to see the doctor at all. The psychologist stood the evidence and told Fabian he would look over it to make certain of its reliability to stand in the presence of the evaluator Sarah's permanent admittance. Fabian was more than fed-up with Sarah. As soon as he reached the gates of his home, he phoned the psychologist, asking about the reliability of the recorded evidence. "RING...RING!" The doctor's phone sounds off. "Yes, go ahead." "It's me...Fabian. Just how soon can you have her admitted?" Fabian asked the doctor. "Well, Fabian I'm afraid that...well, this evidence you provided me with may not be exactly what you may want me to present for anyone's ears to hear." "You got her talking aloud of herself like some insane and crazed animal, don't you, right?" "Owe Yes!' "Well what's the problem?" "The problem is that you recorded Sarah claiming to be speaking to your ex-wife Vanessa. In the conversation Sarah held with herself included the voice transformation from Sarah's voice to the voice of your ex-wife. She went on to share that you and Vanessa use to share many passionate moments in the Jacuzzi." "So you see what I am dealing with then doctor right?" "Not exactly Fabian, the problem is... while Sarah held this conversation throughout; she also mentioned that you were the reason for her death." Fabian's breath was stolen from the news and hung up the phone without any further conscious thinking.

He knew that no one knew the true reason for Vanessa's death, no one except him, not even Sarah. While he sat in the car, staring at the dark mansion and one of the windows Sarah was standing in; he wondered if Sarah had indeed been communicating with Vanessa's spirit, in which even possibly possessed within her from all of the dropped clues that he'd ignored and warned of him before.

Chapter 4

The woman in the bludgeoned water

When he entered into the dark mansion, he found Sarah in the bathroom Jacuzzi once again as usual. The lit candles were of Sarah's as Fabian was the reflection of her through the water, in which she sat perfectly still and entirely compelled as she remained there in the blackened Jacuzzi. When he looked into Sarah's eyes, they were of the fire from the lit and flickered candled. He'd noticed something of the reflection in the ceiling mirror. It seemed to have been of a different figure and movement than that of Sarah's. Fabian looked closer and it appeared to be the naked Vanessa herself, smiling in an evil and enticing way; curling her bloody finger, begging for him to come closer to her. She laughed as she immerged in her own blood bath.

"What's the matter Fabian? You look as if you've seen a dead woman. Take off your clothes and join me inside. Fabian could not decipher what he had seen in this dark room, but he could not help but to think of the sexual orientations she used to give onto him. Fabian considered himself lured into the dark Jacuzzi by his imaginative ability; he saw Sarah as being Vanessa for a moment in a weird unearthly way. Fabian began to slide his hands up Sarah's legs and up into, and pass her flattened stomach, the up to her pointy wet bossism; as they filled his hands with fullness and he was filled with an urge of a pulsating engorgement. He ran his fingers through her hair, and as the candlelight blew in and out, as the last of the wick spared its self, Vanessa's face vanished past Sarah's as the candle went completely out, and she asked… "You missed me?" Fabian jumped out of the Jacuzzi and slid across the floor with his pants in his hands as he flicked the light back on. "YOU CRAZY BITCH! Fabian shouted. "Don't you ever pull such a stunt like this again, ever! Do you understand?" "Well, is that the way you talk to your dead wife? The bludgeoned woman whispered with deceit written in her dark face. We haven't spoken in FOREVER!"

"You know what Sarah? You're completely insane." Fabian stood in from to the bathroom door shivering, as water dripped from his body. "You know Fabian, I know exactly how you treated you little princess Vanessa." "What are your crazy words saying?" "Do you really think that I am talking to myself when you are gone, really? Do you really believe this in your pathetic hallowed heart? She's still here, and she speaks to me all of the time. Sometimes she tells me things of how you use to sexually abuse her, and how crazy you really are. The sexual activities she'd perform for you on the daily. You even had her locked away so that you can sleep with that slut whom called herself Vanessa's friend. You know what? You're a pig. A disgusting pig that only thinks about getting his rocks off every second of a chance you have in a day."

Fabian left out of the Jacuzzi room and through the master bedroom that followed. Sarah stepped out of the Jacuzzi bare naked and headed down the hall after Fabian. Sarah seemed to have gone mad at this very instant of a moment. She'd stomped throughout just about every room of the house bare and still wet from the water that she had not dried from her body, not one drop. "Fabian, I've come back for you! Sarah screamed throughout the mansion as she posed as Vanessa's protégé. Why do you hide from me, my love? Isn't this what you wanted?" At this point,

Sarah truly believed she was "the Vanessa" come back from the dead, and she continued to say "You locked me up and away from society; now I will never leave from your sight, in return for my forever love to you Fabian. Fabian heard Sarah yelling this throughout the mansion and began to wonder if this indeed was his wife Vanessa who has come back for him through Sarah.

She found Fabian in the garden frightened, frantic and paranoid. It was very quiet when she appeared out of ne where. 'There you are, why such a detailed search to find you here?" Fabian was just about out of his wit ends with her. "Look!" Fabian attempted to show her a reflection of herself in the pond as he handed her his towel to cover herself. "You see, it's you! Please let's go to bed. Please! Nothing you've said is true, please believe me Sarah. Come on, let's just go to bed. You should be extremely exhausted by now." There were no further spoken words from Sarah as she followed Fabian to bed. Once they made it back into their bedroom, Sarah approached him. "I'm sorry for frightening you Fabian. Don't you still love me anymore; do I not please you sexually enough. She'd exposed her hard bosoms. Him being a sex fanatic, he gave in and penetrated her with himself. The drunkenness scent fragrance of Vanessa intoxicated him. "Is it enough for you? I'm dripping bloody wet." Fabian broke the penetration between the two, for this line she recited was the very same line that was always said by Vanessa. Suddenly, Sarah's face changed into Vanessa's. 'Is it really you? You've come back for me!" And she replied, "My body is hurting for you. Come inside." Fabian resumed penetrating Vanessa overly and it lasted that night into the next morning.

Fabian began spending most of his time absent and playing hooky from work to extend his short days with Vanessa. Many days was spent with the house phone ringing off the hook in a harassing was until he finally snatched the cord from the wall interior and threw this cellular phone in the out-doors swimming pool. Fabian convinced himself, (the two-faced personality he's developed gradually since the death of his ex-wife)to believe that

Vanessa must have faked her death, and the possibility of Vanessa's spirit over-taking Sarah's didn't quiet register to compute in Fabian's mind for some bizarre reason. But, it still didn't cut the chase; it just didn't explain his hallucinations he believed he was experiencing. The thoughts of him just simply experiencing a bit of an elusive episode didn't make sense and this was not the case if you were to ask him. Fabian truly had lost his mind by now. 'Vanessa!" Fabian showed such an anticipated excitement of interest on his face. 'I should have known it was you whom come back to me. Within my heart, there is only room for you my love." He expressed to Vanessa of how much he'd grown over the years to miss her more and me that his fantasizing over her became stronger and stronger that molded his lustful taste. "Owe the misery I've endured since I've been married to Sarah. You've been away from me for too long Vanessa." He shared his most tempting fantasy of spreading her apart from limb to limb until her secreted liquids exploded onto his tastes per words spoken loudly in many streams of flowing waters.

The fires of lust had built-up within him over the years and x-rated wars were all he could think about of her. This is all that had occupied his mind constantly throughout the day on every day's occasion. Fabian was actually a sex maniac, an out-of-control compulsive ne at that. Fabian became so caught up around Vanessa and his wild sex toys that everything around him in his life was falling apart for the long haul; as he fulfilled his moments behind closed doors with Vanessa and his wild sex animations. His strategic business analysis and hid developed drafts for his up-coming projects all crumbled beneath him. His colleagues were buried in over their heads in drastically measured destructions of kayos that he'd cause. All the company's work tasks became so much in swamped accumulation of fled paper work, to the point where it ran one of his co-workers by the name of Jesse to practically harass Fabian at his own home. On and off Jesse hounded Fabian's home even after the closing of business hours. Even his colleagues went so far as to phone call his immediate relatives to make sure Fabian hadn't endured some type of illness that may be leading to his absence from work. Fabian's co-workers had even held a meeting about his absence. They thought that perhaps he'd just discretely escaped to another one of his trips or vacations without informing anyone in the office again. They searched every document, file and sticky-note pad on his desk even those that were doped of in the trash. They were eager to find some sort of answer to his disappearance. Everyone was confused and concerned for the sake of the company falling apart.

All of Fabian's colleagues from the office joined each other at the bar for further discussion. They complimented each other with drinks as they sat around the bar table discussing work habits since Fabian has been missing. Jesse, one of Fabian's colleagues and main flunkies, claimed to have seen a naked woman standing in the window of the guest room in Fabian's mansion, whom Jesse now claim that the woman seemed to have favored Fabian's ex-wife Vanessa. "Owe, that's bull spit!" Tailor responded. Tailor was actually Fabian's youngest brother whom also worked within the technological corporation as well. Tailor laughed, "Where do you come up with these fairytale bull crap stories? Where do you come from, planet of Freaks?" Everyone gathered in a hysterical moment of laughter.

Very many people did take the story Jesse told to be foolishness garbage, especially, knowing that Jesse is just one of those of many followers of Fabian's associates, who enjoyed the thrills of sex-symbolizing and verbally enslavement to indefinitely define the term "womanizer". So, basically, Jesse's story was over-looked and ignored by many people gathered at the bar table. Mostly everyone there was familiar with the way Jesse talked upon Fabian and they saw him as being pervasive and sexually inappropriate for addressing such news. Tailor, who also enjoyed expressing himself around his brother as a sex involver; if Tailor found this story to be true, he'd do just about anything to see it for himself. When Vanessa was alive, Tailor crazed and lusted deeply over her in the most compulsive of ways ever. When he saw Fabian kissing Vanessa, he always envisioned it being him that Vanessa was kissing, and you can just about imagine all of what else he'd envisioned.

Chapter 5

Spawned eruptions

Back at the mini-mansion, nothing seems to be of a matter or of a worry to Fabian. Only Vanessa mattered to him, mostly just her sex, in which possessed in him into a trans-like state of being. Suddenly, a second transformation in Vanessa began. Just as the myth "vampire" is sensitive to just a glare of daylight, Fabian found himself tripped over the actualization of Vanessa fading from herself and back into Sarah, and then Sarah into Vanessa, then back and forth again, over and over the transformation lasted for like an eternity of time. His vision even became of a blur at times. Sometimes, he even thought he had them both in his presence during his daily routines alone. They were present during meals, bathes, conversations, and even in his bed through the duration of intercourse. Fabian became drunk over the scented fragrance between Sarah and Vanessa both until he became more ill than even before to his greedy stomach. Fabian acted as a madman. He smeared of Vanessa's name over and throughout each and every wall of every standing and cover of the mansion in Sarah's lipstick. The walls began to part and spin off its tracks until he fell to his knees screaming bloody Vanessa! He continued chanting Vanessa's name that night in his sleep until he woke up the next morning from him over drunkenness.

When he woke up, there was a refreshed tone to his atmosphere as if the previous night had never occurred. The morning sun was shining beautifully bright throughout the bedroom window. He headed out of his bedroom doors and down the halls pass the guestroom. The entire pace was spotless and the sound was peaceful. When he made it to the downstairs level, there was an aroma of fresh breakfast slowly simmering and coffee brewing. When he stepped into the kitchen, he saw that it was Vanessa dressed in a pink gown just like an angel over the stove, preparing a morning meal. Fabian exhaled in relief. "Good morning Vanessa, my beautiful angel face!" Oddly Vanessa turned around and questioned, "Vanessa? Do you not remember me – Sarah? Honey, you've been in the bed ill for the past few days now. You must be exhausted." Fabian replied in a panicky fearful state of loosing Vanessa to Sarah once and again as he felt her smooth, raised cheekbones, for her face was still of Vanessa's. "Vanessa it's you, Vanessa! Can't you see your same face, your same body, and the same voice? It's you Vanessa…Can't you see?" Vanessa claiming to be Sarah said, "Now my dear, please sit down and have your breakfast. I'll be cooling down quite quickly very soon. Now please sit down and enjoy your breakfast." Not questioning by much further, Fabian indeed sat down and tended to his morning meal while Vanessa asked Fabian about his duties at his technology company. Fabian began to settle in to somewhat of a clear thought of his career life, while still reflecting on the thought that only Sarah would show concern of his job performance at work. "I promise, tomorrow I'll go in to my job and close some deals that I have not yet done. Okay darling? I just really can't think right at this moment with you referring to yourself as Sarah." Vanessa didn't respond in return, as if she was confused about all the events that had transpired. Or, maybe she was simply suppressing her existence over Sarah's becoming.

Fabian's close sister by the name of Crystal, just so happened to be one of the family members that was contacted by phone from Fabian's business partner who expressed concern about Fabian's consecutive tardiness at the work site. Crystal planned to visit with Fabian at his home, to sex exactly what was keeping Fabian's presence a mystery to everyone. Crystal left multiple voice messages on both his cellular and home phone after receiving only the answering machine. Crystal decided to phone call Tailor, which she and Fabian both shred as their youngest brother in the family. She informed tailor that no one had heard form Fabian, and she is planning on going to his home. Tailor told Crystal, he would tag along after they both confirmed their resemblance in thoughts towards the situation. They both agreed that Fabian would usually, call one of them to send at least a little clue, as he boasted and bragged about if he had a sudden planned vacation. So, for them to not hear anything from Fabian alarmed them both of his disappearance.

Actually, tailor share some very alike characteristics of Fabian's. He sought Fabian to be a man of power and a role model to him as his big brother. So, Tailor's intentions for visiting Fabian's home included a heart full of mixed feelings, especially after finding the story in which Jesse told around the bar table to be hilariously amusing. Tailor was a bit of a sex man himself, with Fabian there to encourage him side by side.

Tailor thought that he'd knew for sure that it wasn't Vanessa in the window naked in which Jesse claimed to have seen. But, he did wonder if this was actually Sarah that Jesse had saw and mistaken as Vanessa. Tailor's mind wondered further alone, and wanted to know how it would be to join in on Sarah's secret kinky fetish. Then he wondered if Fabian was enough to handle her, as Tailor thought how Sarah was only Fabian's second wife and he too knew the real intentions of Fabian's commitment to Sarah - to launch his technology business. Tailor was as well, a sick freak in his own ways that did just about anything to get his kicks off.\

Although Crystal had an extensive history for dearly depending on Fabian from a financial standpoint, she was very concerned and worried about her beloved oldest brother. Crystal wondered if Sarah had neglected Fabian in bed alone, to suffer from some unknown illness and to care for himself. Crystal did not understand what could have been going on, but she could think of a number of things that could've been wrong. Crystal knew that Sarah was usually pretty precise about tending to the care of Fabian. Crystal wondered what the hold-up with the phone call Sarah was never made to Crystal to warn her of the possible conditions in Fabian. When Crystal thought of the excuse Sarah might give to her what Crystal is to confront Sarah of this, the thought engaged Crystal entirely. Stress began to settle into Crystal's mind, so she and Tailor rushed to Fabian and Sarah's mini-mansion at the very instant.

Crystal knew that Fabian was obviously still very deeply in love with Vanessa, even long after the fact that she is now gone, but Crystal didn't know of both the love and] lust Fabian still possessed in him as much as Tailor knew about it. Because Tailor had the same associates and flunkies as his big brother, had heard, shared and saw the entire little dirt secrets each of them all possessed. Especially, the secrets in which of Fabian kept from his wife Sarah was well established by Tailor. So, being that Fabian is the ringleader of their group, he splurged the most information about his life and its luxurious richness of exciting sexual events. Fabian trusted his young brother Tailor, and took him under his wings long time ago when Fabian was still married to Vanessa. After Fabian married Sarah, Fabian left Tailor to run several departments within the company.

Both Tailor and Crystal arrived at the gate entrance of the mini-mansion. When Fabian opened the door, he'd seemed not to have any troubling illnesses at all, which was seen through his blushed cheeks. Crystal held Fabian's reddened cheeks in the palms of her hands. "Are you alright?' "Yes, I am fine and thank you for coming by. And can I assist you with a little advancement sissy?" "Of course not! Where is she?" Who? "Sarah. And don't you try to take up for her Fabian." Tailor interrupted, hoping Fabian will pull him to the side to give him the entire scooped out play. "You've been getting with it huh Fabian?" Crystal gave Tailor the most despicable look. Crystal's only concern was for the wellbeing of her brother, and she was determined to find out the problem by all means necessary. "Why haven't she called me to let me know something about what's been going on around here? You've been ill and she failed to inform the family after all this time of you being absent from work." "It's not her fault. I am the one who unplugged the phone, but if you're wishing to say hello, she is in the kitchen just finishing up with breakfast." Crystal walked into the kitchen. "Hello Sarah.' "Good morning!" Tailor tagged behind Crystal and behind Tailor followed Fabian. Fabian discretely hissed for Tailor's attention, "Spissssss. Come here." Tailor replied in a whisper. "What?" "Do you know Vanessa's been giving me a lot of loving attention around here? Tailor laughed, and now even reflecting n what Jesse had told him before about the lady he'd seen in the window of the mansion, as he visit with Fabian, in his sexual events that had occurred.

Tailor and Fabian stepped inside the kitchen. "Doesn't Vanessa look like a doll face?" Crystal expressed confusion on her face. "Fabian, you should not refer to Sarah by that name. "It's quite fine Crystal. He's been acting sort of strange this entire week now. This is the exact reason he has not been able to tend to work any this week. I just didn't know how to tell you and I deeply apologize. His actions have been very out of the ordinary, and he is way too unfit to return to work at this time.

Crystal was touched on the top of her shoulder and she began to whisper to Crystal in a loud tone, "Do you know that Fabian used my lipstick to smear Vanessa's name on every wall of this house?" She pointed to one of the spots on the wall, where she attempted to wash the lipstick stain off, and then they both returned their eyes back on Fabian in concern. "I apologize for not contacting you, but I have been trying my best with Fabian. I will continue to guide him back to his conscious mental health." Crystal responded to Sarah. "Don't apologize. I am very sorry for your worry. Please just call me if he gets any worst please." Fabian laughed in a hysterical mad man reasoning type of way, "AWWH...OWE!" I know that you're going Vanessa... (He shouted hysterically) You're Messing with MY Mind!" Fabian's reactions scorched Crystal insisted on staying to care for Fabian, but Crystal's assistance was refused and she led Crystal and Tailor the door, then told them both that she will be just fine with Fabian in caring for him alone. "We will be going now, and Sarah don't forget what I've told you. Do not hesitate to call." Before Crystal and Tailor left, Tailor agreed to gather up any files needed to step in and close Fabian's deals back at the office in all of the departments Fabian had concentrated his work when he was well. Tailor was then handed over all of Fabian's files that he had brought home with him and was never completed. Crystal promised to do a follow-up visit by the up-coming weekend. Crystal and Tailor escorted themselves outside the mansion.

Fabian awaited Vanessa's return while he waited back in the lounging area, impatiently tapping his foot to the floor, and amusing himself with her every action. He sat in his black leather chair and his footstool beside him; envisioning Vanessa under his black cloud of smoke destructions, dancing through and beyond the entrapping and merciful heartbeats within the eyes of many chanting tornadoes, and revealing herself as the bride of the unsettled beast himself. Behind the walls of his exterior face, strands of kayos increased his veins within his flesh, with Vanessa pressed beside him. As Vanessa approached back into the lounging area, Fabian's rafts did not rupture off course, as she engulf in his thoughts to exact measurements of his predictions.

"You're good. Owe your good Vanessa. You want me to think your Sarah because you don't want anything to do with me any longer, and you've never wanted to have anything to do with me at all. This is the reason I'd placed you in that psyche institution

– to make certain sure you'll never get away from me, and now you're trying it again! Owe, not this time Vanessa my dear. Shall I punish you like before?" The tone in Fabian's voice was ensuring that he'd indeed gone far over the edge in insanity. She relied. "How about if I make you some nice warm water so that you can take a relaxing bubble bath?" "Cut the shit Vanessa. What was the family reunion scene about?" "Can you just think of how Crystal and Tailor would have interpreted my telling them, I Vanessa, having returned from the dead to reclaim my love for? Don't you realize how they would have thought we were both crazy?" Fabian thought about what she'd just said and came to a brief reasoning. "I'm very sorry my darling sugar sweet heart. You're absolutely right, but Vanessa, how are we going to go on living, telling everyone you're Sarah? You don't think there will be any slips, at someone finding out eventually, do you?" Vanessa replied, "This is something we must keep amongst up only, and away from any and everyone that will be of a threat. You and I both know that no one will ever accept us this way. We must follow through on these plans and never slip up, or else, it will be to an extremely great cost to the both of us." "Now Fabian, we have all eternity to share together, making nothing but explicit, convicted, consensual intimacy excreting beneath the fiber threads." Fabian was appealed by the sound of this from Vanessa again. He began to leap through the links of liquid fires that ruptured of lustful walls within their worlds, and amongst the many scenes, in and out, by far and beyond the mansion's portals developed of Vanessa.

Fabian just didn't still quite understand why sometime, Sarah's face would show in through Vanessa's. When this did happen, Fabian always went on his raging, screeching tantrum fits of tormenting hells fire that last beyond the counts of splits of seconds within time its self; which occurred at least once a day just alike his day-to-day like a turning page sex soap opera, filled with endless run-ons of explicit flicks of him and Vanessa just as he wished.

After an exhausting night of devouring and tasteful love making, the morning sun broke over the sky and into daylight. Vanessa's antidote, a dose of lust had seemed to be wearing of once again, as her enhancing, plump and luscious sexual breast faded back into Sarah's slim and flattened chest. Sarah's completeness in her skin was evident in Fabian's sight.

Chapter 6

Insanities filled with lustful fires

When Fabian saw the change in Vanessa, he'd lost it. He began by forcefully shaking Sarah and shouting, "No you don't Vanessa, don't you leave me here again with Sarah. You know I don't love her anymore, Please Vanessa!" He begged as he wept sobbed tears into his tightly clinched fists to his face. "Why are you doing this to me Vanessa?" Sarah stood over Fabian with fear in both her eyes. Fabian looked up from his wet palms and into Sarah's confused face and asked her, "Why are you still here...WHAT HAVE YOU DONE WITH VANESSA?" He shouted in pure madness, and Sarah answered, "Because I love you Fabian." NOOOOoooooooo, (He Screamed in bloody kayos and then his shouting of cries began to die down) can't you see I love Vanessa more than anything in the world its self?" There was suddenly the most chaotic thought that had entrapped Fabian's mind. Fabian began t wonder what if he was to permanently eliminate Sarah altogether, putting her out of her misery completely. He thought this would resolve Vanessa's disappearance within Sarah's features and her total spirit. Looking into the mirror of Fabian's soul, Sarah could sense what he is thinking about her through his over-grown facial expression of manipulation. It went form a planted fear to an in-merciful desperation that spread over his face entirely. "What are you doing Fabian?" He then began to come after Sarah.

Sarah started to back away from him, but he followed closely towards her until he tripped over the lamp and end table that sat closely besides the guestroom door exit. Sarah picked herself from the floor, and started running down the halls as she screamed hysterically. Sarah continued to attempt escape away from Fabian, on this top level of the mansion until she found a small room that seemed to have never been of any use to anyone. Sarah ran inside and slammed the door locked. "Sarah...my little weak Sarah," Fabian called out Sarah's name, quietly as he tiptoe each and every hall floor by floor and room by room until he found where Sarah was hidden.

"Sarah I'm going to pick your skull past your brain interior masked of matter and filth, until you tell me what you did with Vanessa. Sarah was terrified beyond beliefs until her nervous hands shook uncontrollably as she attempted to securely bolt the door. Her exploded blood vessels raced a marathon around her heart begging in mercy. She screamed with a delirious state-of-shock written across her face that co-responded with her incongruous thinking. "Saaaarraah!" He whispered through the cracks of the door, "Come out come out Barbie. I know Vanessa is in there." Fabian attempted to barge the stubborn door with several striking blows from his shoulder, and began to laugh with acknowledged failure to accomplish to smash the door. "Vanessa?" He shouted. "She's just a hand puppet my sweaty, you show her whose boss here. Vanessa?" Sarah responded, "You're crazy. You've lost it Fabian. Vanessa is dead!" Saliva flown, dripping in response to Fabian's rage of anger and disgust to Sarah's reply as he spoke.

"Open this door Sarah. Open it now. I want my life back and I will have my life back, it this means over your dead body. Fabian shouted and threw another blow to the door. "It's going to be a messy bloody hell for you today." The alteration of Fabian's voice drifted into a gentle and soft tone, as he recited a deadly curse poem to Sarah. "Do you know that they say…when the sun is shining ever so brightly outside, when there's no wind blowing, and burst of showers pore in return, on a day like today, bright, hot but rainy, so you know Sarah?" He begged for a reply as he whispered through the cracks. It means…Lucifer is beating his wife because she made his food too salty. "He began to laugh. "Tis. Tis. Well, he and I have something in common; (he laughed again) we both have high blood pressure! Is this how you think of me Sarah?' He proceeded to ramble on. "I can just see you right now, standing behind this door like a lost, decapitated chicken with than pathetic look on your skimpy face, and those sickened dreadful tears in that run down slinky body of yours that you wish was Vanessa's." He began shouting "Open this door! You Cunt Whore!" "Stop it! Sarah shouted in tears. Her hesitant and exhausted voice in a hick-up of swallowed cries drowned and swelled her throat full as she spoke. "Fabian. You need some help. Please?"

"It's okay if you don't want to open the door, I naturally understand completely. Well, what about if you and I play a little game around here. I'll let you choose. How about that Sarah? Well…I'm waiting. Can't think of anything good? I don't want to propose on you, but you really don't have anywhere else to go anyhow (he laughed) since you can't think of any game in particular, I'll just have to choose it for us. Well I was thinking about a little hide-and-go-seek!" Fabian cracked the biggest pleasured smile on his face in laughter. The game goes a little like this Sarah, let's say… I'm the wolf, and you're the intcy-wintcy little piglet, and on the count of three, this door comes down. Now count with me Sarah, come on. You see it's as easy as one…two…and three (he says in his deviously, hilariously plotted manner), this game is going to be so much fun. Are you ready? Here goes. One…come on Sarah, I know you can do it! Don't make this any worst than it has to be for you…Two! The door couldn't resist the last blow from Fabian's powerful shoulder, and in went the door collapsed to the floor. Are you still hiding Sarah, like a little piglet? OWINK…OWINK SARAH! Fabian spoke to Sarah in a high volume pitched tone as if he were pronouncing to her a royal grand prize winning saying – "Here's Johnny…I'm coming for you Sarah!"

There was a small bed and side table that occupied this useless room. Fabian looked under the bed and then proceeded to the closet. Fabian began to laugh as he observed the slight movement in the large velvet drapes. Fabian began to insult Sarah. "I know you're behind those drapes Sarah. You know what gave you away? Your disgusting body is so thin, pale, unattractive and… LIFELESSNESS." Sarah franticly surrendered herself from her hiding place so that she can ruin him from nearing any further towards her. "Please!" Sarah stepped from behind the drapes. "Owe no. (Fabian responded) You're gonna get it now. Why are you still her e in the presence of my domain? You're not welcomed her e any longer Sarah. I've warned you already. I've made this clear to you and now this serious, serious, serious problem Sarah has got to end right now. Fabian started towards Sarah, he held her neck with his masculine hands. "Say goodbye Sarah. You're not still here are Sarah? He asked as he tightened his grip, squeezing tighter and tighter around her neck. Sarah strangled for air and Fabian began to cry in joy. "Vanessa? Vanessa, my love, Vanessa wake up! Vanessa?" Sarah could no longer speak, but lucky her, she was able to loosen from Fabian's strong hold and escape the extreme struggle between them two.

Sarah ran down the hall, back into the bedroom and securely locked the door, but Fabian came following close on to her path in a rage of vengeance in Vanessa's death. Sarah knew that she had to think of a quick plan to escape Fabian's insanities of obstruction. Sarah thought that the telephone should be in perfect functional use in this small room. She quickly moved towards the phone as her life depended desperately on it, in hopes of a solid ring tone, but the tone was dropped to a silence. Fabian had cut the lines from a back-up fuse box that was in a dark corner of the hallway, in which was left there pacifically for emergency purposes. Sarah was beyond disturbed to learn that Fabian had but the phone lines had prevented her from telephoning Crystal to inform her of Fabian's attempts to strangle her to death. Sarah had not a clue as to what her next escape route would be; and so she meditated on the thought, as she eliminated all odds against her that insisted to stand in her way.

As Sarah contemplated on her escape, Fabian was analyzing an assumption of Sarah's thought to precise predictions. 'You're not as smart as you think you are Sarah. I have you out-beat when it comes to thinking ahead!" Fabian rushed into a side room where he'd remembered stashing a safety key laid flatly still in the bottom of a drawer. Fabian began down the stairs, out the back door and into the shed near the outside greenhouse. Fabian then grabbed his old ladder and planted it under the bedroom window. Fabian headed up the sturdy ladder, took the key to the bared window and completely sealed it locked, and Sarah then tried to pry the bedroom door from its hedges, but it would not give in to Sarah's weak pulls.

Reality steps in, and Sarah knows that it may all soon come to an end, and possibly be all over for her, the resistance from Vanessa's coming spirit demolishes at this point, and she wonders what Fabian may be up to next. Her strength to fight him off of her slowly dies. The thought of his raft destruction tore through her flesh as he headed back down the ladder. Her frigid body remained standing in the middle of the floor helpless and oppressed over the conspiracy. Her mental order refused logic of the entire situation that transpired, in which led her into the abandoned room and into the state of inconclusive.

Fabian went back inside of his domains and stomped through and up into the stairs, then down into the halls where Sarah had been hiding away from him like a frightened and entrapped alienated experimental species. Fabian began to shout as he preyed on poor Sarah, "You know Sarah? You should appreciate my masterminded abilities; my skills of thinking since they are above and beyond those in which you can control, your immature mental mind set can't process these types of things adequately. You were always weak and incompatible. You overly exhaust yourself just attempting to think on my level. Just give it up Sarah. You can't win this one against me. Once I've made my mind up, that's it. It's all over for you. Make the most of your choices right now. You either give yourself over to Vanessa, or give yourself up and over to me in suffering the consequences. Make your choice."

He took the back of the hammer t the door and began slowly un-prying the nails from the door, and saying to Sarah in a mockery way, "Now what are you to do Sarah, and where are you to go/ You can scream all you want and no one will ever hear you through all this land surrounding us." The last nail came unhooked from the door, and their Sarah was standing in the middle of this small room shaking in terror. "Is this how you want me to remember you, pleading and begging of mercy?" Fabian dragged of Sarah in to the Jacuzzi room. "Alright Fabian you win. Vanessa's all yours, I can't continue this way. All I ever wanted was for you to love me the way you use to, but I now see that this will never happen between us again. If it makes you happy for Vanessa to take complete hold of me; my entire being here on earth with you, then she's all yours. I just wanted us to be happy together. So, I see this is the only way?" "Get into the tub Sarah!" "Tell me how you did it. "Did what?" "Don't play games Sarah. I know about this room. This is the place she mostly introduce herself to you. My precious time is ticking away as we speak in these riddles, so don't you pretend to be lost now. You've spoken to her in this mirror as you mentioned before, so do it, bring her back to me now. I'm really growing more impatient as you sit here in my presence." Sarah wanted to be Vanessa so bad, so that Fabian would love her and give her the acknowledgment that was no longer of him when he dropped the ball. Fabian thought Sarah was so obsessed about the concept of being Vanessa only to entice him in conceiving his baby through Vanessa. Only, Sarah was indeed playing with fire and found Vanessa's spirit actually lurking in this room that Vanessa once shared with Fabian. Her transitioning into the realm of realm of actual time, cried out to be free through Sarah in revenge of her death. Sarah demonstrated her love and wished for Fabian through her irrelevant expressions and body gestures under her breath of unspoken words through the mist of the air of her love for him. Sarah proceeded to light the surrounded candles, as she sat in the tub, while it filled with her sleek body and over her lost soul. Sarah sat in the tub and watched in the mirror patiently, with Fabian hovering over the two souls of both Sarah and Vanessa measuring the relations of quantity in devour.

Chapter 7

Vanessa's bludgeoned rage

The onset of Vanessa's appearance entranced Fabian into the realms of liquid fires she promised to consume of him. His mind exploded in her thoughts and the walls emerged while it rained bloody hell from the mirrors of the ceiling platform Vanessa laid in. He could no longer see of Sarah, but through her was Vanessa as she rose from the waters engulfed of red fires to indulge in Fabian. Vanessa spun Fabian in a thousand storms of lustful acts then spat him out like mucus waster. "Forever you'll be mine!" Vanessa said to him, as he dazed in to her blazing horrific contempt eye matter and her fiery red hair. Vanessa gave herself to him like none ever imagined, and caught dust to his soul in her spoken words, of his name down and into this throat, she confronted him. Teasing trace marks of her raft smeared his forehead and stuck like matted delusions. She made love to him overly in her horrific states of tournaments for him and beyond his capacitie4s to unmask of her. He was forced to expose of his filthiness, and every day she laid pressed in his arms for forever on to him.

She slavered his weakness on to her tongue and it melt into her flesh, growing over him in dominant revelations. He looked no further of her as she plunged into his soul. His secret mysteries washed out then tricked from forms of sinful fountains of lakes and drowned his swallowed taste. The hunger for her died drastically slow into non-existent time, captured by her unearthliness, and his regretful thoughts ran witty of a thousand lapses within empty space, but his thirst still out-grew his hunger, and he died in her over and over again.

Jesse found himself in suspicion, and caused him to reflect back to the night be saw the lady in the window, an image like that of Vanessa's. Jesse realized not one individual believed what he claimed to have seen, but he was persistent to find out the truth to what he indeed saw on this particular dark and mysterious night. Since that night, Jesse had been creeping around the house on a regular basis and just so happened to be standing outside watching from afar. To his surprise, Jesse saw Fabian locking bedroom window bars and had not a clue as to what Fabian's conditions were, or even his intentions to doing such an odd and unusual act. For the mansion was surrounded five hundred acres of land. It was always peaceful and quiet to exact sound. Jesse could feel in his gut that something strange and out of the ordinary was of Fabian. Jesse continued to prowl and ease-drop around the house, but could not link his suspicions together, his final straw of meditated patients was drawn and he was ready to pronounce himself into the home of Fabian's and Sarah.

Jesse was indeed a flunky of Fabian's, but it was to his career growth potential, and he never under-estimated Fabian's swindler ways, not to the least bit. The sealed windows and doors hindered Jesse from entering into the house. One swipe to the front door lock, and it instantly came slightly opened. The house was pitched black, and he could hear nothing of either Fabian or Sarah's presence in the huge mansion. As Jesse investigated his way through the mansion, the splashing of water alarmed Jesse that someone was upstairs. He tipped toed up every inch of each step until he reached the top railing and slipped on some water Sarah missed earlier. Fabian didn't hear the streak of a fall from

Jesse's tennis shoes, and Jesse traced the foot tracks down into the blackened hall and into Fabian's chaotic aftermath.

Jesse approached the bedroom to find Fabian and Sarah both soaking wet and unconscious with Fabian laid over Sarah on the bathroom floor of the Jacuzzi room. Jesse tried the house phone, but saw it was completely dead and had no idea that I tin fact had been cut by Fabian. He noticed a dead pulse in Sarah's respiration and her paled skin. He then guided Fabian from on top of Sarah's limp body. Jesse attempted CPR to resuscitate her. Suddenly, she coughed up the water that was left on her lungs. Jesse didn't know what to think of all of this mess, but it didn't look very assuring if Fabian was to try to prove his innocence. "No, you're taking her from me!" Fabian shouted in his dazed and delirious unconscious state of deep sleep. Jesse stood over Fabian as he spoke in his sleep of Vanessa's name; and convinced that Fabian most certainly have lost total control of his manipulative mind. Jesse placed Sarah on his back and down into the dark and slippery hall, than down the stairs and out of the front door while Fabian yelled in his sleep, "Vanessa come back! Don't you love me anymore… VANESSSSAAA! VANESSSSAAA!" He called in his sleep.

Chapter 8

Secluded corruptions

The next morning, Sarah telephoned Crystal from Jesse's home. Sarah informed her of the situation that had transpired between her and Fabian the previous night, and Sarah insisted that Crystal revisited the mansion to check the condition of which Fabian was left to himself, Crystal stated that she would give Sarah the word to immediately enter into the home, and to shortly return Sarah a phone call to either, reinstate Sarah's warnings or to give her the head ups and reassure Sarah that it was sage to reenter the mansion for retrieval of her remains within the home.

After Sarah's hanging up the phone with Crystal, she home phoned Stacey to instruct him to meet her at the mansion in assisting her with vacating the home, but there were not an answer and unfortunately, she was only able to reach the his voice mail. She decided to try contacting him again, and after so many attempts of only reaching his message system, after plenty of consecutive times, Jesse began to wonder of the importance in her persistence. So he asked of Sarah, and she refused to give him any revealing information for her intents. "Sarah, I have all the time on my hands and I'll put my entire day to side jus to help

you with your personal matters you may be facing. You don't have
to continue to go through this alone.

I know this is more than difficult for you to cope with. You're
a very strong woman, and I am here for you as a friend it you need
me. Just know that, please Sarah. I'm here for you." Sarah looked
at Jesse in a relieved way, and then she continued to proceed in
her repetitive phone calling until she reached mental anguish
within herself. One last try and Sarah came to the conclusion
to finally leave Stacey a voice message, explaining every detailed
structure of the events occurrence that prevailed over the night
and throughout the leading moments of day.

The phone rang. Jesse and Sarah both hound it in anticipation
of it being Crystal. Hand to hand, they met, with Jesse's upper
hand on hers. Sarah answered the phone. "Yes?" It was Crystal,
and as she spoke through the phone to Sarah, Jesse tried his best
to listen in on the conversation, but the words were too scrambled,
and Sarah ended the conversation and sat the phone back on the
receiver. "What is it?" Jesse Asked. Crystal had in fact, gone over
to check on Fabian, but claimed the door was locked and she had
no way of seeing his actual condition for herself.

Sarah paced in the middle of the floor, not knowing the
outcome of the situation. Jesse insisted for Sarah to get some rest
over night, and first thing come morning, he would escort her
into the house, but Sarah insisted in going alone and sequentially
attempted to contact Stacey. "I really don't think it is a very good
idea to go back into that mansion all alone." Sarah was against
the idea of Jesse tagging along with her, at this point, she was
perfectly aware of the consequences she had to face by going back
into her home alone. "Do you think you should at least get the
police involved? Sarah seemed to be ensured of herself, "No, not at
all." She answered as she peacefully concentrated on relaxing her
tensed body. Sarah wondered out of curiosity, "Jesse...do you find
me to be attractive? I mean, not as your type of dating preference,
but just as an attractive woman?" Jesse didn't have to ask any

further of Sarah's reasons behind the question, for he could just about read through her mind. "Fabian was a monster. He never appreciated you, and now he has to live with himself and face up to the consequences of never getting completely over Vanessa."

Sarah lay on Jesse's sofa as he watched Sarah's limp and exhausted body become more and more relaxed. Her breathing became slow and steady until she was completely asleep. Jesse took his place in his single spaced bed and slept for the entire night. While Jesse slept, Sarah had awakened herself from a disturbing and terrible dream. The dream was of Fabian, winning possession over the mansion and all that she'd worked for to help build everything that molded the relationship. Sarah reached over to the phone that lay on Jesse's table and began to call Stacey once more as she whispered through the receiver and onto his voice system before she quietly hung up. She accomplished to sneak pass Jesse's while he slept, grabbed with his car keys form beside his bed, then proceeded to tip toe out his home.

It was a long dark and risky drive back to the mansion. Sarah even had her moments when she had to move over to the edge of the road from her confusion state of being; lost where she saw herself seeing illusions of spirit-like images within figures off side the road and within dark shadows that surrounded the woods. Sarah recomposed herself and remained to realize it was only she and the woods alone. She then preceded her long ride back to the mansion. Sarah spotted a bright light, in which became blinding as she approached in the direction of the secluded mansion. Once she pasted sensory lights that lit up around the entire mansion in warrant of someone's arrival; she had approached the tall black iron gates that surrounded the mansion. Sarah comes to a halt in uncertainty of her mission. Sarah proceeded inside the black iron gate until she reached the front entrance to the door, and noticed the automotive gate locked by Fabian behind her. Sarah was terrified out of her wits. Fabian had been watching Sarah from a dark window the entire time of her arrival to the dark and crept mansion. Plotted on his face was a dark and cold energy, written over it, one of an insanely driven manic anticipating on Sarah's return all alone. Sarah consistently stared in Fabian's empty face and noticed him holding a shinny object, but she could not distinguish it. Fabian stood up out of his chair, and Sarah's facial expression dropped in wrenching bloody fear. She could clearly see in his hinds, a large axe as he disappeared into the dark room that he stood in with the most deceitful and evil of grins on his face.

Sarah's heart raced out of hell's fires and skipped into her intolerable veins throughout her body in dysfunctional coordination. Her mind escaped onto the horrific consequences of unimaginable bloody shedding, and her body broke down in shock and did not respond to move at all. Sarah decided to quickly escape in a dexterous transitioning manner; moving to the back of the mansion where she would sometimes leave the gated door unlocked for herself that led to the pond, but, she found it to be locked. Sarah could hear Fabian coming from the front door yelling, "There's nowhere for you to run to out here Sarah. Here I come!" Sarah quietly eased into the greenhouse and hid away under the greenery in some extra stock of soil.

Meanwhile, Fabian followed his hungry footsteps in vengeance of Vanessa until he reached back of the mansion and checked the locked door to make certain that it was securely locked from Sarah's escape. Fabian came to the conclusion that Sarah must have hidden in the greenhouse. He began raging and cursing in vein of Sarah's work and tending she'd done to her greenhouse, expressing his disgust for her occupation. He included mentioning how pathetic it was to him as he shouted how he never ever loved her. Fabian took the back of the axe to the glass and began bursting and shattering every window from its frame fixture. Sarah remained hidden under the immature plants, trying her best to stay silent as she heard Fabian stepping on particles of broken glass as he entered into the greenhouse. "I know you're in here Sarah. So, what made you come back?" Fabian analyzed each corner and dark area where Sarah could have hidden herself.

He observed some plants that had a sway of motion belonging to it from when Sarah brushed up against it, trying to hide from Fabian. He began to laugh. "You will sleep in that dirt you're hiding in." Sarah hopelessly surrendered from behind the soil and showed herself in his presence once again. "It's me...Vanessa."

Fabian stepped closer to touch the tears that rolled down one side of her cheeks, and she felt his lips with her fingers, as they drew each other in for a kiss. 'I miss you so much Fabian, this is why I've come back...it's me...Vanessa." Fabian gently touched her soft face with one hand, but she noticed that he was still holding the axle just so slightly. She felt his psychotic face with both her palms of her hands. She then moved both of her hands down towards his left hand and on top of the blade bar. "Why don't you put this thing away before you hurt yourself?' Fabian looked into her and showed a slight concern in his deep eyes before he struck her to the ground. "Do you think that I don't know how Vanessa's lips feel from your disgusting moist kiss?" Fabian started after Sarah once more, and she cut the thighs of both her legs trying to push herself out the busted glass window to escape from Fabian. Sarah began to run back towards the inside of the mansion, but managed to fall into the swimming pool instead. "Tiss,Tiss, Tiss Sarah." Fabian said as he stood over the pool nodding his head; watching Sarah flop around in it gasping for air. "You clumsy, selfish whore."

Fabian watched poor Sarah nearly drown. He proceeded towards the hose and clicked the switch, causing the eater protector cover to run. He then left to go back into the house, and then went into the lounging area and sat in his black leather ottoman with his feet up top of his footrest, with the axle laid across his lap in both his hands. As he sits totally elated, he thinks to wait awhile for Sarah to catch water and drown, his plans are to check the pool for her dead body, and patiently wait on the final lasting appearance of Vanessa through the flesh that was so precious to him in preserving for his long lost love in Sarah. Fabian was very reassured in confidence with closure as he cracked a huge smile.

Meanwhile, as Fabian sits, Sarah catches the outlining of the pool covering just before it closes. Sarah's fingers gripped the edges of the cover and climbed to the surface of the pool. Several moments after, as Fabian sat in his chair; he glanced over to the side of him and noticed how the pool was still slightly revealed under the pool cover. He decided now was the perfect time to check the pool for Vanessa's coming. With his axe laid to one side, in one hand; he un-flicked the switch to check the inside of the pool, then checked over to the outskirts of it. The pool began to uncover and he stood over it with his image reflection glistening in the over-riding of the ripples formed by the heavy blow of the wind. Fabian's eyes enlarged as he was shocked more than ever, and grew into a raging driven maniac. Sarah's body was gone! He jumped inside the pool with his axle; swam to the bottom then to the top several times over and again repeatedly, checking the entire pool for he remains, until her reached the thought of her being gone enlightened his reality. He floated on top of the water with the axle in his hands, when he noticed Sarah standing inside their mansion in front of the closed patio door. Sarah stood at the door and locked it as Fabian came out of the water drenched wet with his shinny axe in his hands; not taking his dark, shadowy stare off of Sarah for one second.

Sarah backed-up as Fabian headed towards her until she was no longer in his sight. She heard the glass brake and she ran up the stairs where she attempted to reconnect the cut phone lines, but there was no hope. "You're a fool for coming back!" Fabian yelled form down into the lounging room. Sarah panicked as she hid in the dark corner not knowing which way to turn, and Fabian caught u with her and entrapped her like prey. Fabian took Sarah by the hair and dragged her back into the Jacuzzi where he wanted to finish her off. He stripped the clothing from her head to toe. He repeatedly dipped Sarah's head under the blackened water, Sarah screamed but no one could hear her, and every time she did manage to loudly scream to the top of her lungs, water filled and swallowed her throat. Fabian repeated this until Sarah was unconscious. Fabian was positive that if was the end for Sarah's limp and lifeless body. He propped Sarah's wet, limp body on the side of the Jacuzzi and re-lit all of the candles that surrounded her. He then flicked the light switch off in hopes that Vanessa would appear once and for all.

Fabian patiently guarded over the body that was once full of Sarah's liveliness; his delirious mindset observed movement in her. He welcomed his reincarnated experiment thought of Vanessa's coming. 'Vanessa!' Fabian grabbed a towel and began clearing the water from her nose and mouth. She stood up in her naked, wet body and exposed was her breast. Fabian flicker them of her drenched bosoms and slavers them with his slithered tongue, then down to her navel. She stands over him with her red fiery hair, demeaning him with her empty bloody blackened eyes, as he worshiped the ground she walked. Fabian picked her curvaceous body up and placed her on the soft pillow-top, then plunged into her flesh as she yearned for his. His world spun drunken into sodden dimensions of organisms trusted from her and grew in throbbing desperations; extensively penetrating her throughout, from the course of his engorged masculinity design. The secretion from his mouth fell over her in glut hydration and to the period of exhaustion. Fabian was so grateful of Vanessa's resurrection until he became a slave onto her. He took her inside the bathroom and ran her the most luxurious bubble bath, cleansing her entire fame, from her high cheek bones to her pouty lips. He pore the filled bubbled sponge over her fiery hair and took her wet body out of the tub, patting her dry before placing her back into bed then said, "My Princess!" He left her in bed as he prepared her breakfast. He noticed how her voice was dropped and she had no words for him at all. His demented thoughts perceived her as dead as he proceeded to finger feed her fruits.

Meanwhile, Stacey was just turning in form a long night spent in his home office in front of the computer, investigating files form back at the job. There had been a generous amount of money missing from numerous accounts. He was driven to figure out exactly where all the money and funds had disappeared to. Early on that night, before he began his research, he'd figured to turn the ringers off all his phones to eliminate any distractions and interruptions of any kind in order to complete this important investigation. After the entire night of observing and comparing files, he found no reliable evidence. Now will be the time to check his messages, he thought for any possible clue. As he goes through his messages, he realizes that numerous of phone calls were made in attempts to reach him but not one message was left. As he prepared for bed, he thought he may have heard a young woman's voice early on his voice system. He stopped everything he was doing to replay the message. It was Sarah. Her voice alarmed him while he listened to her whispering the message that he could not decipher.

Stacey sat at the front of his bed; reflecting back to the day Sarah had given him a tour through her and Fabian's mansion. Stacey could remember Fabian being perfectly calm on that day about the situation. Stacey was sure it was enough to infuriate him. Stacey looked over his shoulder to his wife sound asleep in their bed and wondered what she'd think if she'd found out about what was going on with him and Sarah. He considered the thought of the consequences before leaving his wife in bed to go into Fabian's home that night to confront Fabian of his transgressions towards Sarah. Stacey assumed at this point that his odds out-weighed him. Stacey kissed his sleeping wife on her forehead and left out and away from his home.

As he drove closer and closer to Sarah and Fabian's mansion, he could see just a hint of light from the changing of the sky which was of the only light in the pitch black that swallowed him in, but it was still not enough to turn away from the dark, secluded and lost mansion. Stacey's conscious alarmed him of the dangers he would possibly and most likely to incur from his un-welcoming approach. As he reached the gates of this dark shadow and disturbing place, he decided to call the detectives to aware them of the case, but they had no reason for their involvement of intruding, based on the lack of accurate information Stacey could provide. They instructed him to call emergency if anything threatening was o occur. Stacey sat inside the car, looking up at the mansion and wondering about Fabian's potential raging destruction. He knew that if he did experience any inflicting harm by Fabian; it would practically take forever for help to arrive just to rescue him and Sarah, being that the closest police station from Stacey's home alone was over fifty miles away, and then from his home to the mansion was approximately two hundred miles in distance.

Chapter 9

Stirred Madness

The winds were howling and the tree leaves were blowing in every direction from its branches. Stacey knew a terrible storm was approaching near. He hesitated, as he eased his car past the iron-gates, thinking of his means of defense to protect himself against Fabian. Stacey parked his car near the entrance to the mansion and stepped out of his car to feel the dead and warrant air to his skin. He stood there in place for quite some time, dazing into the mansion before feeling an unwanted presence behind him. Just as he turned around t see what the presence may have been, Fabian, being the psychotic maniac he is, came up from behind Stacey and struck him with the back of the axle, to the side of Stacey's head, then watched him fall helplessly to the ground. Fabian took the axe and posted it into the standing of a nearby tree, dragged of Stacey's body into the house, up the stairs and into the guest room where he hogged tied Stacey and left him to the floor. Fabian proceeded back outside, released the axe from the tree then went back inside and into the top level of the mansion. Fabian sat in the middle of the blackened hallway, where he laid the axle against his head, meditating over what he should do with Stacey's remains after the actual bloody act.

Fabian furiously stormed into the guest room, stomping through the cracks and crescents of the floor, shaving it from its entire foundation, then slammed the guest room door behind him. Fabian approached Stacey with the most disgusted look on his face as he asked, 'You're trying to screw my lovely Vanessa, just as you did Sarah… in my house, as I sat in the lounging are like some kind of pathetic mutt day, eating scraps for the freaking dinner table while you and Sarah "tour" around our home." He held the precisely sharpened blade of the axe to Stacey's genitals; Fabian positioned Stacey for a manageable planted decapitation. He held the axe in an upper position. "Fabian?" he heard the softened voice of his forever love calling for him, and he ran for her like a lost child. He rushed to her as she lay still in bed. "Yes Vanessa?" "What's going on out there?" "Nothing, just get yourself some beauty rest, my love." "But Fabian, I need you here with me." She enticed Fabian to stay and make love to her one last time. Fabian was occupied with her, while Stacey slightly gathered himself from the concussion, but found the rope to be tied into a figure eight knot around his neck and it was obviously too tight to escape. Stacey thought, as long as he could scoot his body across the floor without Fabian hearing him, he will be able to find something sharp to cut the rope and reach his pocket phone to call for emergency. It was to his limited ability to execute his plans without Fabian knowing by the noise he'd make as Stacey thought. Stacey raised his self from the floor and managed to glide the doorknob in between his fingers and quietly turned it open. He then scooted himself down into the hall until he reached an empty room. His blurred sight spotted through the open door – a shinny object of some sort. He could not distinguish what the object could have been, but after reaching it, he found it to be a letter opener that had fallen to the floor. He managed to cut himself from the tied rope then called the emergency station for help.

Fabian's throbbed penetration ceased, but it only motivated him to execute his prior plans for Stacey unknown disappearance from anyone ever finding out. Fabian lay sunken in the bed as he stared into the ceiling meditating with axle to the side of the bed. The thought of Stacey making explicitly passionate love to Sarah in his Jacuzzi, infuriate him and sent him on a disastrous raging, threatening the parallelism between him and Vanessa. Fabian, with his one tracked mind, picked the axle up from its core and stomped down into the pitched blackened halls of the mansion, then into the guestroom to find Stacey gone. Pits of hell engulfed in Fabian's torturous eyes, and the sound of the beast himself , moved drastically fast throughout each and every single room of the upper level; thrashing furniture from wall to wall, breaking every piece from its pending structure.

As Fabian trashed the mansion, Stacey slid into Fabian's bedroom and saw Sarah laid limply throws over the bed, but could not distinguish if it was indeed Sarah or a figure of another woman like her. Stacey was so destruct by her horrific appearance that he stood over her naked body in shock that seemed t last forever. Her hair had a hint of hire to it, and her face was painted with an array of non-richly tented hues of pastel-like paints that shaded near the passing of death. Her skin shrunken into creases within its self, and her expression drowned in tearful shame and horror outside herself. Stacey was held in contempt within the moment. Fabian creeps immediately behind Stacey and catches him observing Sarah's non-existent limbs. "Do you like what you see?" Fabian asked. "Fabian what have you done? What are you, some sort of monster? ANTICRIST! LUCIPHER HIMSELF!" Fabian replied, "There is no more of Sarah…I know what you want. I know why you come back here Stacey." The madness on Fabian's face grew in endless rage. "You barge into my domains like price charming? You want to sleep with Vanessa just as you did with Sarah, now don't you?"

Fabian could hear the police sirens counting off from a far and closing in on him. Fabian's mad and eventful thinking preoccupied him in vengeance and rage, growing over him by countless seconds. "Get in there." Fabian pointed to the Jacuzzi, "this is where it all began, and this is where it all will end. Right here right now." Stacey gradually stepped into the dark room and into the cold water, shivering cold, as Fabian forced him deeper inside. Fabian turned to the non-existent body of Sarah's. "You and I shall never be apart. We shall live forever together my lovely Vanessa.

The deputy, along with his men sped pass the iron gates and to the mansion, barely stopping their brakes in time, to avoid spinning off the pathway of the tracks, as they sharply turned their wheels at a complete stop. The chief and the cops rushed into the mansion. There Fabian could hear them searching the entire bottom level for him. Once the men reached the lounging area, they noticed the water tracings on the marble floor. Half of the team slit up into two groups for a thorough search of the mansion. The first group found themselves contemplating over the swimming pool, then the greenhouse, where they discovered Sarah's bloody tracks. The men gathered and rushed to find the sheriff to inform him of their findings. The chief deputy and his men marched to the second level of the mansion, with the detective closely behind their footsteps. They approached the top level, with indications of a suspected struggle to show for, and all the evidence of Fabian's revengeful rage was in the deluded air.

The teams again, split into the dark halls, searching every single obstructed object in every room. Once blow and down cam e the bedroom door. There stood Fabian just about to take a strike to Stacey's neck with his axle. The sharpened axe blade gleamed in mid air at the spare of Stacey's life. The deputy yelled. "Stop!" The police officers guns are drawn. Fabian dropped the axle and fell to his knees and surrendered to them. Stacey appointed the detective to the Jacuzzi room; while the mansion was entirely spoken of the horrific acts of a monstrous manic, in attempts to a massive bloody spree, but the stunned detective couldn't quite pace his fingers on what to call it for sure, "Premeditated Murder, "Crazed Manic gone psychotic over the Passion for a whither love"? The question haunted the detective. The Jacuzzi room looked as though someone had been drowned to death, and there was water and traces of blood everywhere from the swimming pool t the bedroom.

The detective posted himself over the bed, "What is your name Miss?" Under her dry and dehydrated tongue, she answered in a whisper…"Vanessa!" Stacey was blown way in devastation, and whispered to the detective to search the Jacuzzi room, where he would find closure that would end his investigation. The detective analyzed the evidence and the statement Stacey had given in practically closed the case onset of the detective's findings.

Meanwhile, the paramedics checked the mysterious woman's body, and saw if oddly strange that she had not occur any serious bodily harm, other than the cut she had on the inner thigh of both her legs. "My name is Vanessa. My name is Vanessa!" She repeated over and over again in a manic trans-delusional state. At the trauma center, she was thoroughly evaluated, then placed under close observation for seven consecutive days. After a week had come to past, the doctors discharge her home. Stacey took his time away from his wife just to check in on her on the regular basis, in hopes she would recuperate and come back to herself.

Stacey experienced her raging events of claiming to be Vanessa in an egotistic manner, even to bring up Fabian's name constantly throughout several moments. What she didn't project is that, Fabian would be locked away for a very long time for the crimes he'd commit. Day in and day out, Stacey indwelled into her mind over and over again, until Stacey began to see a little improvement in her.

In the mean time, Fabian dwelled in his psychosis state of mind, plotting in his undisputed revenge, smearing his clear finger prints over every glass standing of this four wall psychiatric confinement, as he blazed himself of Vanessa's damned spirit that smothered his mind. What Fabian didn't realize before – is the reason for Vanessa making passionate and consensual love to him within Sarah, was to deceit of him in his pervasive ways; bringing her spirit to an actual breath of life to spend with him, while she suspended her love for him in vengeance of her death and the endured pain she experienced when she was alive. Fabian was so blinded under lust of her name that all he could ever think about of her last days she lived was the interludes sex she gave onto him. So much of him wishing Sarah was she, he finally got what he wished for, but only not exactly the way he thought.

You see, the entire concept of Vanessa's presence was just all in his head to begin with. Sarah played along with the entire ordeal of enslaving his thoughts of Vanessa. The day Sarah invited Stacey over to the mansion; as Fabian sat in the lounging area, and Sarah gave Stacey the tour of the bedroom is when it happened. Sarah indeed invited Stacey into the Jacuzzi room, but did not have an affair with him as Fabian actually thought as he waited patiently on his wife to return. Instead, Sarah and Stacey black mailed Fabian. Stacey implanted a spyware and image transmitter device into the mirror of the Jacuzzi room that very instant specifically to monitor Fabian's out-raged reactions and flawed behaviors of Vanessa's pseudo image. Sarah needed some sort of evidence to convict Fabian. These were her plans to regain recognition of ownership of the company Fabian ran alone as he abused his statue of authority. When Sarah proposed the deal to Stacey, he was more than willing to settle a deal. Being that, Stacey also had shared accounts and privileges to them, in which he sat back and watched Fabian misuse the system and treat to his personal accounts.

With Stacey's assistance, Sarah was able t leave all her past troubling conditions behind. She moved out of the mansion and bought a condo in the inner city of New York, and hired an agent to put the mansion on the market. Sarah was granted legal rights over every possession in which her and Fabian shared during the course of their marriage, and the secret experience of Vanessa's after life still remains a mystery.

From this day forth Sarah meditates incisively. All of what she sees is an out-skit of placing scattered puzzled pieces into a resolution to design the whole picture. Now Sarah sits in her authoritative black leather chair in conveyance to her royalties and out of the hands of the idolized and manipulative deceiver. She drifts into her immortalized thinking, weighing the odds behind its truth in existence; compromising Vanessa's spirit and reality, as she thumbs her skinny efficacious fingers in between her pendulum. She thinks of how contempt Vanessa's spirit has to be in the closure of her death to spend many live with Fabian; suspending vengeance upon him in his ruining he casted down on her when she was alive. Sarah dazed out into the scenery of her luxurious business office into the sky and takes a deep breath, "Ah, if it wasn't for Vanessa...how my faith lays within both palms of the forever unknown hands."

Sarah knows that selling the mansion will be a task on hand. The secluded mansion still remains to be empty. Some people say that during their tour to purchase the home, they hear swishes of water from the base level of the mansion, a sound like someone bathing. Some even claim to hear wet footsteps walking the second floor, and an image of a naked woman standing in the window of the guestroom; awaiting for someone. Sarah can only think of one thing it may be...Vanessa, soaking in the hot tub as she drifts in and out of Fabian's psychotic, episodic, and lustful mind! Revisiting the mansion for old time sake, cleansing herself from the torturous liquids full of sinful bloody lakes of fire that she unleashes upon him while penetrating his thoughts for all eternities to come, laid upon him as a curse from the other side.

Fabian was a womanizing man who had became of himself, and whom attempted every single last element he could, from every aspect of sinful, deadly cons against those who tried to put a stop to him and Vanessa's bloody love life. He really had a great affect on those who favored his trades.

Turns up, Sarah had a greater degree of clout from Fabian's colleagues as it turns out. He flaked by porting numbers with all odds against him. Even the psyche doctor rendered his attention and services to Sarah; accepting every single last evident Sarah and Stacey presented to have Fabian committed in to a psyche ward. Fabian lacked the qualities needed to run the business after-all. Sarah now, sits at her desk back at the office; thinking how Fabian finally received his ranted wishes and just deserts to spend eternity with Vanessa. He can now spend his life with Vanessa in his own sick and twisted mind, devouring in Vanessa's death kisses that pierced his illusive mind every day so forth until the end of eternity; entangling with and labeled as officially insane.

Printed in the United States
By Bookmasters